The River Calls
By: Ron Shepherd

Global Video Marketing
& Graphic Design
Publishing Division

Second printing
Email: peaceriverbooks@ronshepherd.com
Website: www.ronshepherd.com

ISBN: 0-9769455-3-3
PUBLISHED BY GLOBAL VIDEO MARKETING
PUBLISHING DIVISION
www.globalvideomarketing.com
Minnesota

Printed in the United States of America

To my sister Helen,
my encourager.

Table of Contents

Prologue

My name is Dr. Matthew Andrews. I have a small office overlooking the Bigfork River here in rural northern Minnesota. I was a writer many years ago when I was much younger, back in the days when I had to pound hard on the Smith Corona keys to make an impression on the paper. Today things are quite a bit different. I can write a letter, and it will come up as green characters on the monitor as I type.

I wanted to write about all of the things that my old friend Wil Morgan and I had done so many years ago when I was young. Northern Minnesota back then was a wild and wonderful place, full of the many characters that made this country legend. The numerous stories that Wil related to me of his hunting years, and his life on the Bigfork River, along with the experiences we shared, were full of excitement, danger, and sometimes humor.

So in my dimly lit office in the evenings, I rest my fingers on the keys and watch as the lives of many good and gentle people unfold in emerald green letters.

Chapter 1: The Savage Hunter

Two gray timber wolves waited on a granite outcrop for Wil Morgan to die and make their job a bit easier. They had eaten nothing for three days. The cold winds of October ruffled the long hair on the big males neck, making him look even larger that he really was.

These were unusually lean times for the pair, and winter wasn't far off. Earlier that morning, four of them rushed the man, but he killed the two young males. The female once again moved in closer to him. The man's blood scent made her bold. She crept in low to the ground on alert for any movement. When she got within striking distance, the man moaned in pain, and she quickly retreated to a safer distance.

Wil had been hunting deer to feed his family and, in a moment of inattention, stepped into an old rusted bear trap. The sudden pain to his right leg took him by surprise, and the trap pulled him down to the ground, holding him fast with forty pounds of rusted steel. As he fell, his 45-70 government rifle flew from his hand and landed far enough away as to be out of his reach. Over the span of many years, the trap chain had grown deeply into the tree that held it, and there was little chance to cut it free. He tried hard to open the jaws of the trap, but each attempt brought such great pain that he nearly passed out. Inch long steel teeth dug deeply into his now broken leg.

On the first night, he was able to gather some fresh fallen snow for the moisture, but the next days sun took what snow was left. He could go for quite some time without food, but his fever made him extremely desperate for water. He gave a fleeting thought to cutting off his leg. Deep inside he knew that he could do it, but a man with one leg had little or no chance to survive in this hard and demanding country, much less support a family.

Wil found a nearby piece of balsam wood and pounded it inside the jaws of the trap. He needed to get blood flowing to his now cold foot. Each time he struck the wood, he could feel his head spin and his consciousness start to fade.

Before it got too dark, he scratched for pine straw to cover himself. On the second night, he dragged the bodies of the two young wolves he had killed close to him for warmth.

For three days he tried to get free of the trap. Weakness and thirst took their toll. At times, he felt that he was in a place where reality and nightmare meet, and he was uncertain as to which side of that divide he was on.

Wil Morgan was a hunter of many years. He faced the dangers of the outdoors nearly every day, but he never thought too much about it. He had some close calls, but he held the edge because he was tougher than this land he called home. He thought of his wife and boy back at the cabin and wondered if they had sent someone to look for him and how they could survive there on the river without him.

The pair of wolves became emboldened by hunger. In this small battlefield in the pine forest, there was an epic war being waged, and the wolves would surely die if they didn't eat soon. The fearsome eyes of the two predators met for a moment, and the male slowly moved back into the darkness of the woods. The female stayed where she was, barking at the man occasionally, attempting to keep his attention. In a few moments, the female stopped her distraction and locked eyes with the man. He stared intently back at her, his coal black eyes trying hard to pierce her thoughts. She broke off the staring match, turning her head away so she didn't have to look at him.

The big male circled around behind the man, moving slowly and silently. In a powerful, lightning fast attack the two wolves were on top of him. Wil cut a wide swath in the air with his knife, but came up empty. The powerful male grabbed him by the shoulder, and the other had a grip on his free leg. They were strong predators getting closer to a long awaited meal. Wil fought bravely, but weakened by thirst and loss of blood, he could do little to ward off the attack.

The big male shifted his grip to get close to the man's throat where the lifeblood ran near the surface. Wil could feel the end coming closer. There was some pain and some weakness and then a feeling of peaceful darkness. It was as if this were happening to someone else, and he was just watching. From a distance he felt the great animals shaking him.

A shot rang out, and the big male lost his powerful grip, falling dead on top of Wil. The female ran into the woods, leaving behind what was once a powerful family of predators.

Chief Bustikogan had stopped in to see his old friend Wil. Wil's wife told of how he hadn't returned from a trip into the woods hunting for deer. Not wanting to waste time, Busti gathered together a few supplies and left the river, tracking Wil into the big pines. At times he lost the trail and had to circle to pick it up again. He had been on the path for many hours and was moving slowly, concentrating, trying to think of where Wil put each foot as he walked along. He looked for the smallest of details, like an overturned pebble or a piece of a broken pine needle. At times he had to get down on the ground and crawl on his hands and knees to find what he was looking for. The trail was difficult, but not impossible for this native of the pine forest. Daylight gave way to evening, and the tracking was becoming harder because of the fading light. Busti built a small fire to pass the night in the pines. He heard the sound of timber wolves attacking something. He thought for a moment to let the wolves make their kill, but he wondered if it might not be his friend Wil that was their intended meal.

The Indian grabbed his rifle and moved quickly through the tall timber, toward the sound of wolves making a savage killing. He looked ahead into the fading light and saw two wolves attacking a man on the ground. He raised his rifle and fired at the one nearest the man's head. The big wolf yelped briefly and fell dead. The other released its death grip and ran silently into the darkness. As he approached the man on the ground, he saw that it was Wil, bleeding and nearly dead. He turned his head and squinted in the near darkness, trying to see who it was that saved him. Chief Bustikogan of the White Oak Band and Wil shared a brief moment of recognition and relief. All that Wil could say was said in his eyes.

His mouth was parched dry from two days without water. Busti gave him a drink and went to work trying to open the trap. He pounded a hardwood wedge between the jaws, and with each attempt, Wil nearly passed out in pain. He held a small stick in his mouth and bit down hard. Within very few minutes, Wil felt the steel trap starting to release its hold on him, and soon Busti was tending his wounds. The wolves had actually done little damage to him because of his heavy leather coat, but not the trap's jaws. Busti wrapped several pieces of birch bark around the leg and secured them with rawhide. This immobilized the leg and gave Wil some degree of relief.

They were a long distance from Wil's home, and Busti thought that the best thing to do was to go back and get a horse. He left Wil alone again in the big pine forest and headed to the cabin to get what he needed. A trip of several miles at night was a hard trail for any man, but for his old friend, Busti did what needed to be done. Wil sat by the small fire for several hours, and by mornings first light, Busti was back with a horse, water, and food. Wil ate some and drank more water. Busti built a travois out of blankets and poles, and Wil climbed on for a bumpy ride home. Each step the horse took brought more pain until finally Wil closed his eyes, losing consciousness.

His leg healed slowly, and by mid February of 1927, he was back to some hunting and the chores to keep the farm running as before. Busti stayed the winter with Wil until he healed and could do most things alone. His wife cooked and cared for them until one day Busti took Wil's hand and said good-bye. The two friends parted company, and in deep gratitude, Wil told him to come back any time he could. The words to this old friend came from deep inside his heart.

Chapter 2: Migrations

Matt Andrews picked his way along slowly in the dark, listening to the many thousands of Canada geese out in the open water. He nearly stumbled on something and realized that it was a man wearing a dark coat, huddled down near a stump.

"Damn. I sure didn't see you there." said Matt.

"No harm done. Guess I should have said something when I saw you walking toward me."

Matt walked on for a short distance and decided that he had found an excellent spot to hunt from. He sat down in the dark, glad that he hadn't stepped on a moose, as he nearly did last year. The dike was strewn with many tree stumps and large boulders, so it was easy to miss things.

Daybreak and the years first goose hunt were only about a half hour away. He could see the sky starting to turn red in the east. Matt had waited impatiently for this since way last year. The fire of the hunt burned brightly inside him.

The geese were starting to talk a bit more excitedly and soon they were heading to the stubble fields for their breakfast. It was October, 1942, and there were more waterfowl than there had been in many years. The first bunch of geese leaving the water sounded like on old freight train, with a loud rushing sort of clamor that grew louder and louder.

The first flock started to come toward where the men were crouched down in the reeds, waiting. They were in great bunches now, and one flock flew toward them, staying a bit lower than the rest. Matt's shotgun came up smoothly, and the charge of high base number fours erupted from his old smoothbore with a solid kick to his shoulder. The confidence that he had in his shooting abilities was immediately dashed when the birds kept flying after his shot. He quickly put in a fresh shell and brought the single shot 12 gauge to his shoulder, but before he could squeeze the trigger again, a shot went off nearby to his right. A big Canada goose crumpled and fell only thirty feet from Matt. The old man in the dark coat nodded and grinned. That was a long shot for him.

That fall morning, the two men shot a lot of game. The weather was cold and miserable. The Canadian wind took all the warmth Matt could generate, and his flask of blackberry brandy did little to help ward off the chill. Ducks and geese by the thousands were on the move ahead of some yet unseen storm.

In a couple hours, the shoot was over, and the excitement of the opening morning began to wane. The fall sky was warming with brilliant oranges and reds without hardly a whisper of wind to move the cattails. All had turned calm, and Matt was enjoying being there, just being alive. This was a good time to pick up his birds and head back to the car. As he looked for his last one, the old man approached and claimed his goose. He wore an old canvas coat that looked like it had been used for more years than Matt had been alive. He had a dark complexion and large bushy eyebrows that ran in two broad arcs across his forehead. He had a salt and pepper beard, mostly salt, and an old slouch hat that gave him a weathered appearance. There wasn't much of a smile on his face, but it was enough to show a sparkling gold tooth. He extended his hand.

"I'm Wil Morgan."

He had a deep gravely voice that matched him well.

"Nice to meet you, Wil. I'm Matt Andrews. That was some nice shooting this morning. I can't believe I missed that first shot."

"Guess I've been doing this for quite some time now. You from around here?"

"No. I come up here for the hunting. This has to be the prettiest place I've ever seen, and there always seems to be a lot of birds."

The two hunters sat down on a large log and watched the many hundreds of high flying geese migrating through. They flew along in formation, and as they got over open water, they flipped on their backs and dropped like falling snow. They righted themselves, glided a short way, and did it all over again. Matt hadn't seen that before.

"I come up here mostly to recharge my batteries. I live in

Minneapolis, and it's hard to relax there."

Matt thought about what it was like back in the city. Weekday mornings he got up early to have coffee and read the morning paper. He liked to see the sun come up, even if it was filtered through several layers of acrid smoke from the factories. He got in the tub and scrubbed up from top to bottom and shaved his face so that he looked presentable to the world, but more importantly to his boss, the head of the hospital. Some days he wanted to forget shaving altogether and go to work in his oldest most comfortable pants.

"What kind of work are you in?"

"I'm a doctor and occasionally a writer when I get the time."

"That sounds like a pretty good life to me. Are you married?"

That was another thing that gave him reason to think back toward Minneapolis. He got up early each day to go to work and got home late from a very long day of taking care of his many patients. At times he went for an entire week without seeing his wife. The big old brick and stone house sometimes looked like no one lived in it. She had her social life, and there was little time set aside for him.

"Yup. I'm married, but no kids yet. You been up here before?"

"I've hunted here for quite a few years now, since I was a young kid, I guess. We used to come in with horses and wagons and stay until our supplies ran out."

"When would that have been?"

"Well, that was a long time ago now. Something how the years can slip away. Most times I'd bring my boy with me. He turned out to be quite a good hunter. It seemed like he had a kind of natural feel for the outdoors. He paid close attention to the wind direction and the colors of the sky and saw lots of things I didn't even notice."

"Is he here with you this year?"

"No. We lost him at Pearl Harbor on the U.S.S. Arizona."

He got a kind of far away look on his face.

"Sometimes I really get to missing him, especially at sunset when I'm watching the last of the day go by. I know that he's with me then, but it's scant comfort when I think of all those hunting trips we had together. He sure was a fun kid."

Matt thought for a bit and hoped that he hadn't stuck his foot in his mouth.

"Where you camped at?" asked Matt.

"Into that far tree line, about a mile from here I guess. Have you set your camp yet?"

"No. I'm still looking for a good spot."

He was hoping that Wil would ask him to share a campsite. Sometimes in the evening it was nice to have someone to talk to.

"Why don't you set up near my digs? There's good water, high ground, and an open spot for your tent. You wouldn't know how to cook, would you? I haven't had a good meal in quite a while."

"I can cook some if it comes in a can."

The old man laughed a bit and said that if they put their heads together, he didn't think either of them would starve. His eyes sparked and flashed when he laughed.

It sounded like a pretty good idea to Matt, so he agreed to share a fire with the old man. He didn't know it at the time, but that old jackpine savage and him would, as time went by, become close friends. It seemed that you make a large pile of acquaintances over the course of a lifetime, but darned few real friends.

Later on, as the evening sun dropped toward the bare oak branches and the temperature fell, the camp was set, and the water was drawn for the next morning's coffee. The ducks were having quite a conversation out in the open water, and they heard many flocks of geese flying over the Roseau River area. They cleaned all the ducks and geese and packed them in salt.

Supper was in the planning stages, and for Matt, it was usually a matter of heating up a couple sausages, but Wil had beat him to it. As he approached the fire pit, he saw a goose turning on a spit. Wil turned it a quarter turn and brushed it with bacon fat. He waited a minute or two and did it again. It was beautiful. The aroma was making Matt's taste buds turn handsprings. It came to him that the old man had been fooling him. He was an excellent cook. Wil tended that goose like he was painting a masterpiece.

Matt sat down near the fire, and Wil offered him the first sip out of his newly opened jug of whiskey, an honor usually reserved for close friends. The drink burned like the fires of hell, but he didn't want to make a face in front of this grizzled old gentleman.

"How do you like living in the big city?"

"It's not so terrible, I guess. Sometimes I get in such a hurry to make money that a whole month will go by before I know it. I see patients every day and send them bills. Sometimes they pay, and sometimes they don't, but I guess if I was in it to get rich, I'd have to move to Chicago. A family that I was doctoring, one time, paid me with a calf. Bet I would have had trouble putting that in the bank."

They both laughed.

"Everything seems to go at a pretty fast pace. I guess that's why I need to come up here to relax."

"Looks to me like you forget to eat most of the time too. You could use a few pounds on your bones," said Wil.

"As the men talked, a large flock of sandhill cranes came winging by in the darkness. These were big birds, and their rasping voices echoed back and forth in the little clearing. As they crossed in front of the full moon, the hunters could see their long necks stretched southward.

"Now there goes a flock of the best tasting birds on the Roseau. They're hard to get a shot at, though. They have pretty good eyes, not like mine. These old eyes are starting to get a bit fuzzy at times."

"Looks to me like you see a lot better than I do by the number of birds you shot today."

The old man grinned in acceptance.

"What's it like living up here?"

"I would guess that it's a bit different than what you're used to. We stay busy most of the time with the garden and farming, but we take time to smell the flowers and go fishing, too."

"What about in the fall?"

"That's a pretty busy time of year for us, too." Wil said. "There's always a lot of meat to put up for the winter and about eight or ten cords of good dry hardwood. The wife cans all our greens and vegetables. If the garden produces good, we try to put away three or four hundred pounds of spuds, too. Winter's hard on us all, and sometimes we can't get to town for a whole month at a time. That's pretty tough on a woman."

Wil took off his hat and scratched his bald head.

"Do you ever think of moving to town?"

"No. I don't think I could ever do that. My family and I were raised there on the river, and all the old ones are buried there, too. I guess we'll stay there until the good Lord calls us home."

The fire was crackling a bit, as the goose fat dripped off the bird. The smells of campfire, swamp, and fall seemed to make the evening into what Matt had waited for since way last year. For now, though, it was a time to relax and try to put the city of Minneapolis as far to the back of his thoughts as possible. He had to get back to the city in a few days. There were appointments to keep and people to make well. His boss would be counting the minutes until his freshly shaved face turned up in the operating room.

Wil got to his feet and stood over the now smoldering fire assessing the quality of his evening presentation. The Canada goose was at last done to perfection. It didn't look too bad, considering the fact that he didn't know how to cook.

Wil took it off the fire and set it onto a clean, newly split, half log. He pulled out a long shiny knife from its sheath and carved off a steaming hunk. He nodded at Matt, and he in turn, with the same knife, sliced a large piece of breast meat and put it on a blue enameled steel plate.

"There's not much to this surgery stuff." Wil said with a slight twinkle in his eye.

"Nope. Nothing to it. Now, lets see you stitch it back up and make it fly south for the winter."

They both laughed hard.

The flavor of the roasted Canada goose was wonderful. It was smoky and salty and tasted like it was cooked in heaven for sure. It was far better fare than the fried sausages that Matt had thought to make for a meal. Wil handed him some hard bread and butter, and that made the meal complete. The men were silent. In due time, there was not much left but bones and greasy fingers. Wil threw the used up carcass and the log into the flames.

The young doctor looked at Wil for a while, trying to figure him out. He was a very good natured and polite man and seemed to be generous to a fault.

"What was hunting like here when you were a kid?"

"I guess I never thought about it too much. We came here to put up meat for the winter. It was a lot of fun for a kid, though. I must have been pretty young when I started coming here. In fact, I can't remember not doing it. The older ones did most of the shooting, and the kids helped with the cleaning. We packed the ducks and geese in salt, and the venison was mostly dried in thin strips, and if it was cold enough, we hung the meat in the shade to freeze. We sure ate good though. Come nighttime we rolled up in our wool blankets and slept under the wagons. Those were sure some good times. When I was about fifteen, we got our first tent, and that made a big difference. When the winter snow made an early appearance, we brushed it off the tent and went on about our business."

Wil went inside his tent and pulled out a jug. He handed it to Matt. The young doctor took a polite swallow and didn't even make a face. It was Wil's turn. He tipped up the jug, gulping down several swallows. He corked the jug once more and set it back away from the fire.

"The hunting back then was a lot more serious than it is now, and we were much more careful about our shots. Money was pretty scarce, so I didn't dare waste a shell, or Dad was right on me for throwing away good money."

"There were a lot of good times back then, too. After all the work was done each day and our bellies were filled, we listened to the men tell stories around the campfire. I remember hearing my Uncle John tell about what he did one time when he got lost in the woods. He said that he built a signal fire so the searchers could find him, and after spending the night in the woods anyway, he decided to build one a bit bigger, about forty acres. They howled with laughter as if they hadn't heard it before. It seemed that the first liar didn't stand a chance with this gang, and each story was surpassed by the following one and so on deep into the night. Us kids sat under the wagons listening wide-eyed to all the stories, not quite knowing which ones to believe."

The two men sat quietly for a while, digesting the conversation.

"I haven't really hunted very many years, but I sure do enjoy going when I can. Medical school took most all of my time for quite a few years, and the new job at the hospital took a bit more. Have you ever hunted the Dakotas for geese?"

"Done that a lot of times, and we had a bunch of good hunts. An old fellow by the name of Ernie Barten was one of my hunting partners. He never married, and when I met him, he was already nearly eighty years old and an amazing marksman with a shotgun. He wore a beautiful red velvet tam to cover his shiny bald head and had been accused of fathering fully half of the children in the Upper Balsam area. He could shoot a Hun and have it cleaned and in his pocket before it was time to shoot again."

He paused for a bit to gather his thoughts.

"One evening, Ernie and I were standing near a big slough, trying to decide where to be at first light. Ernie looked up and nodded off toward the north. There, as the sun was showing its last bright rays of daylight, were geese. Now, I'm not talking about a flock of geese, I mean geese by the tens of thousands. There were snows, Canadas, and blues, and some I had never even seen before. They stretched from the north as far as you could see to the south as far as you could dream. The geese were in full migration and had no intention of stopping anywhere near us. We sat down on the ground and watched. It continued deep into the night and all the next day. Even old Ernie with his many years under his belt hadn't seen such a sight. The next day, the geese kept going, but the ducks made up for it by giving us some good shooting. The weather turned cold, and we were standing in the water almost to the top of our waders. Ernie pointed to my left, and there, coming right at us, were five bluebills. I crouched low, and as they came in close enough, I fired one shot, and they all hit the water at the same time. I thought that I was pretty darned good, but after a short while, Ernie let me know that they had dived into the water, and I hadn't hit a single one. It kind of deflated my puffed up chest a bit. He was right, though. Not a single duck lay dead on the water. I would say that, at that particular time in my life, I still had quite a bit to learn."

"That sounds like you had quite a trip."

"Yup. We had a lot of them like that, lots of good memories. All through my life, it's been like storing things in a locked box. Each memory is put inside for safekeeping, and every once in a while, I'll unlock the old box and take out one or two, look them over, roll them around inside my head, and put them back inside. Sometimes when I'm all alone on the river, I take out a hunting trip from many years ago or maybe a special Sunday dinner. It has a way of keeping my life fresh."

The two sat and watched the fire for a while, enjoying the warmth, and the way the sparks sailed upwards and were swallowed up by the darkness.

"What was it like when you were a kid?"

"It was pretty tough for a kid where I grew up."

Matt said no more and sat there watching the fire. He seemed to be unsure of what or how much to say. He had only known Wil for a very few hours, but he felt a closeness and trust and wasn't sure where it came from. He pushed his hat back on his head and looked Wil straight in the eye.

"Life was tough for me as a kid. Alcohol seemed to have a great hold on my parents, and it got stronger as time went by. School was about the best part of my life. I remember one day when I was about thirteen, some kids asked me if we were going duck hunting on Saturday. I lied and said that my dad and I were planning on going hunting for ducks, and we always got a lot where we went. The kids laughed and said that I hadn't even held a shotgun in my whole life. They started in about Pop being a drunk. Well, that got me pretty mad, and I figured that I better do something, or it would get worse. I picked out the biggest kid with the biggest mouth. I took a big swing and caught him square on the nose. The kid went down hard at about the same time the teacher came around the corner. I was in serious trouble and had to stay after school. The teacher gave me a note to take home, telling about what a terrible bully I was. In a way, that note made me kind of proud, but on the other hand, I had to show it to my folks."

"How did you handle the problem?"

"I sure took my time walking home that day. I came in the back door, and there was Pop, asleep at the kitchen table with the usual empty whiskey bottle keeping him company. I knew that if he saw the note now, he'd beat me bad. I went back outside and tore the note up and threw it in the garbage. As it turned out, the teacher never did say anything more about it, and I saved myself from a beating."

"Did you and your dad ever do much together?"

"No. It always seemed that they looked on me as being a real inconvenience. We never hunted or fished together, but I didn't want my friends to know. I figured that when I grew up, I'd have a son and do all the things I never got to do with him."

Matt got a pretty serious look on his face, and Wil knew that it was about time to call it a day.

"Well, Matt, I think that I'm about ready to hit the sack. I'm not as young as I used to be, and 5:00 comes pretty early in these parts. My knee says that we're in for a change in the weather, too, probably some snow by morning, and that will really put the birds on the move. It should be a pretty good day for us."

Without another word, Wil stood and walked over to Matt. He slapped him on the back and disappeared into his tent. The fire was still going strong. Matt threw a few small chunks of wood on the fire and sat down to watch it die. The brilliant colors were nearly hypnotic, and in a very short time, he was sound asleep.

In a couple hours, Matt awoke to see the flames gone and fluffy new snow settling on him. He stood to go into his tent and found that darkness had stolen nearly all his sight. It was blacker than the inside of a cow, and it took a while before he could make out the form of his tent. He settled in for the night, covered with a large heavy feather tick for warmth. The temperature had dropped, and the water for coffee would surely be frozen solid by morning.

Sleep came easily for Matt that night. It wasn't at all like the big city with its sirens and trolley cars running at all hours. The sound of his own beating heart came as a surprise to him. He had never heard it before except through a stethoscope. There was a great silence in their hunting camp that night, and he could feel his soul stirring, recharging.

Chapter 3: The Elk Hunt

The crackling sound of the campfire awoke Matt with a start as the flames danced back and forth on the wall of his tent. The old man had built a large fire to warm himself. Two inches of fluffy snow had accumulated during the night, and everything was frozen solid. Wil shoveled around the fire pit and cleared an area in front of his tent. It was still pretty dark, but there was work to be done.

The blue steel coffee pot bubbled and hissed with each wasted drop. The thick smoke curled upwards and disappeared into the inky darkness.

Matt's head was still full of cobwebs and the remnants of last nights' whiskey. He wasn't quite ready to get out from under his blankets. As he lay there, he thought about back home in the city and the feeling of lying next to his wife before the alarm clock sounded. Occasionally, she reached over him and turned it off. His thoughts wandered for a moment. He, at times, had speculated about his own sanity for getting up so early and considered going back to sleep. He was here for the hunt though, and that is what he was going to do. This was going to be a great day, and the birds were out there waiting for him.

"Good morning, Wil. That coffee sure smells great."

"Morning. Grab a cup. It tastes pretty good, too."

Matt poured a cup of steaming hot coffee and immediately burned his lip for being in too much of a hurry. He grabbed the big cast iron frying pan from the hook on a nearby oak tree and got ready to fry up some side pork. He filled the big pan with meat and salted it. Then came the pepper. He liked his side pork nearly blackened with pepper. He set the pan on the grate, and in a short while it came to life sending a spray of fat into the fire. As it flared up, Matt could see Wil's many years in the lines and creases on his face. He had incredibly black eyes that looked alive in the flames.

These two were an unlikely pair with one a survivor and one a doctor. One was educated in many distant and expensive schools and one was educated in the back woods. One was toughened by many years of hard work, and the other was soft from city life. Each man had his strengths and weaknesses, but together, they each seemed stronger.

After the side pork was done, it was time to cook the eggs. Matt got the grease hot again and cracked two eggs for each of them. He swished the pan around, and the grease rolled back and forth. The eggs were done perfectly with a nice lace edge to them. Wil accepted his breakfast with a smile and grabbed a piece of bread to sop up the yolk. Matt's breakfast was identical except that he loaded his with pepper.

After breakfast, few words passed between them, and each had his chores to do. As daylight neared, they were at the same spot that they had hunted the day before. This day was different though. There wasn't the usual grumbling of geese out on the open water. They waited in the near darkness, not making a sound, and then there came the familiar whistling sound of bluebills speeding by in the near darkness. Every once in a while there was the fluttering sound of wing hitting wing. Matt and Wil strained to see them but only caught glimpses as they winged toward the gradually lightening sunrise. They came in large flocks with little time in between them. It was as if all the ducks in the world were here at once.

When Wil fired the first shot, it startled Matt. He was so intent on watching the ducks that he had forgotten what he was there for. He lifted his 12 gauge to his shoulder and fired at the first good target. It splashed in the water and gave him a great rush of satisfaction. He quickly put in another shell and shouldered the gun, but this time he missed, and the bluebills kept going with no break in flight. They were headed for open water, and nothing short of lead was going to stop them. Wil was spacing his shots widely, and with each blast, there was the corresponding splash of a duck striking water. In time the shooting slowed down to nothing, and Matt wandered over to see how Wil had done.

"This is the best shoot I have ever had." Matt said.

"Oh, it gets a lot better than this. Sometimes the winds of early November will get to blowing, and all the ducks left on Lake Winnipeg will leave at the same time. When they come through, it sure is a sight. You shoot until you get tired."

"I sure would like to see that sometime."

By 10:00 that morning, the migrating ducks were nearly done flying, and it was time to pick up the morning's harvest. Between the two hunters, there was a grand total of twenty-seven ducks to clean.

When they got back to camp, Wil pulled out the black steel pot filled with paraffin and bees wax. He placed it close to the flames, and the wax slowly started to melt. After each duck was plucked, he immersed it in the wax and hung it to cool. The wax was peeled off and thrown back into the pot to melt again. The pinfeathers and down were lifted from the melted wax with a scoop. It was a very efficient way to take care of a lot of game.

Matt cleaned the birds and packed them in salt, all but four which were for their dinner. He looked over at Wil and noticed that the old man had a soft smile on his face. Matt wondered what Wil was thinking.

As they put the finishing touches on the birds, the sky darkened. The snow from last night had melted, and the ground was back to the color of dead grass. It was early October, and it would snow a few more times before it finally stayed on the ground. The campfire was built up in readiness to roast ducks. Wil had been busy over behind the tent, and when he reappeared, he had the ducks ready for the fire. He stuffed them with dried apples and prunes. This time he arranged them each on their own stick so that they tilted in toward the fire. Every once in a while, Wil rotated them so that they wouldn't burn. The aroma that filled their hunting camp would have put a New York chef to thinking of a new vocation. This was a very slow method of roasting, and the aroma was surely making them both hungry. Wil tended the ducks carefully, like they were his personal friends. The old man was a wonderful cook, and as he basted the ducks with side pork fat, they sizzled and danced on their sticks.

After an extremely long wait, it was time to eat. Wil took down their blue enameled plates, and on each, he placed two delicately browned ducks. He poured a small amount of sherry over them for additional flavor. He put a piece of bread on the plates, and that was their dinner. At first bite it was evident that the old man had done it again. The flavor was fantastic, and both men ate in silence.

When they were done, Wil stood up and with a soft belch announced that he had finished his dinner. He wiped his face on his coat sleeve and grinned at Matt. The coffee was very strong and was a fitting end to a fantastic meal.

"Where in the world did you ever learn to cook like that?" asked Matt.

"I guess after cooking this many meals for this many years, you have to get a little better at it."

They both laughed.

That night it seemed that the small circle of fire was the center of their universe. All that they could see at the moment was what the small campfire could illuminate, and the world dropped off sharply as the darkness consumed it. This was their whole world for the night. They had full bellies and someone to talk to. No one could ask for more.

"What's on your mind for tomorrow Wil?"

"Well, I'm not dead sure, but I think we should get some venison drying. I made a rack last year, and it's still over there against that large popple tree. I need to take a couple deer before the snow shuts us down. I'll make a good smoky fire and dry it well."

"I didn't bring a rifle with me, but I did bring some slugs, so I guess that will have to do."

"I've hunted nearly everything that there is with slugs, and they never failed me yet. You have to be a bit more careful about the range."

The evening fire crackled and popped in the stillness. All their work was done for the day.

"Have you ever hunted elk?"

The old man got a kind of twinkle in his eye, and a small wisp of a smile crept across his weathered face. There was little in life that he liked more than elk hunting in the Rocky Mountains. He had killed several in his many years, and he unlocked the box to share some of his finest memories with Matt.

"There was a time when all that mattered to me was the hunt. I would have done nearly anything to be up in the high country looking for that really big bull. The air was good and clean, and there were a lot of animals. The trip there took nearly a week, and the roads were pretty bad, too. Denver was a big city back then, with a huge number of people, so we always had to stop and see how the rich folks lived. They even had indoor privies. Prices were really high on everything, and a steak cost over a dollar, so we ate mostly what we brought with us.

"We looked around for a few hours, and it made us glad to be living back on the river. We got back in the car and headed up into the hills. We chased the rivers and railroads, as they wound further and further into the mountains. When the darkness settled in on us, we stopped for the night. The headlights on them old cars weren't too good, and it would have been easy to hit one of those big boulders that fell off the mountains. Some were nearly as big as a car.

At daylight we started off again, heading for the high country. The trip really wore us out because the roads were so rough. When we went through some of the higher passes, the boy got a bit scared, but he tried hard not to let is show. The drop was even a bit steep for me sometimes. When you're raised in the flat country of Minnesota, you're not used to such things.

As we got closer to where we wanted to hunt, we got more excited. These were wonderful times for us both.

We made camp at around eleven thousand feet, and the snows hadn't started there yet, but it wouldn't be long. Again, it seemed to be a matter of getting meat for the family, but the hunt itself was pretty important too. Sometimes we sat watching the show, listening to the coyotes calling back and forth across the miles.

The first morning there we spent listening to the big bulls bellowing across the valleys. They were intent on gathering a harem of cows and defending them from the young bulls. Sometimes it was pretty easy to fool them. We would sit behind a windfall or big rock and give out a kind of screeching whine. The old bulls thought there was a new gal in the neighborhood and come to investigate. Then the work began.

Our camp was set in a depression near the road. There was a small flat area that faced south, and we had our campfire going right away to cook some much needed lunch and coffee. While I was getting it ready, the boy took a hike to the top of a steep hill behind us. He wasn't gone very long when I saw him hiking back toward camp. He had a pretty good sized smile on his face, and as soon as he got near me, he went into that hunters' whisper. That's the kind of talk where you keep your voice real low so that the person you're talking to can't hardly even hear you. He was a most serious hunter, and that blond hair and freckles made him look even younger than he was.

The boy said that he had seen two cows and a small bull a mile or so from their camp. They were bedded on the south side of a hill soaking up the sunshine. He grinned inside. That boy could sneak up on anything.

I got out the big skillet and started to fry up some potatoes and onions. The boy ate his share and more. It seemed to take quite a bit of food to keep him going all day. We went back to planning the hunt for the next day. I figured that he wanted to go back to where he saw those three today, and I sure wasn't wrong. The kid was really excited. I was pretty sure, as well, that there would be a lot of animals on that hillside next morning. We had to be darned careful about the wind, though. In these parts it could come from all four directions at the same time. Nothing messed up a stalk faster than that.

We finished our meal and pretty much spent the rest of the day getting the camp in order for the weeks hunting. We had to put up quite a bit of firewood and carry lots of water from the stream. We unloaded the car and got the trailer set back out of the way. We put up a big canvas tarp to keep the rain off us if the mountain weather decided to turn sour.

We got out our guns and cleaned them up for the hunt the next day. I ran a piece of rawhide through the barrel and pulled an oiled rag through the bore. I oiled and dried the receiver. I raised the 45-70 to my shoulder, imagining the thrill of sighting down on a big bull. For me, the thrill of the hunt was as strong as when I was a much younger man. The boy took great pains to make sure that his gun was cleaned to perfection. We sat there talking for a long time, and he kept the gun across his legs the whole time, like he didn't quite want to put it away.

Evening came to the mountain and with it a complete sky full of sparkling stars. The sight was humbling to both of us. Looking at such a display made us feel pretty small. We laid back on the ground and watched the show. My eyes were nearly as good as the kid's so I picked out a part of the night sky and tried to imagine what it looked like much farther away and deeper, much deeper. The harder I looked, the farther I could see. The thought of distance without end was pretty hard to swallow. Every once in a while, a shooting star lit up a small piece of the night sky. It was quite an experience.

Morning found the weather drastically different than the night before. There was no wind in the mountains at all, and the temperature was way below freezing.

After we ate a couple bites of breakfast, we headed out together. He was fifteen years old and had a lust for the hunt that reminded me of my earlier years. We each found a spot about fifty yards apart. Night gave way to the morning sun, and the boy started to cow call. He was good at it from a winter of practicing at home that nearly drove his ma crazy.

Within an hour, we heard a big bull answer and hunkered down to wait him out. The boy was intent on looking to where the bull bellowed last. We heard him again, and this time he sounded somewhat closer. He took out his bugle call and gave a long series of bellows, whistles, and grunts. He was looking down the heavily wooded hill where the bull had last been heard. I watched the boy staring intently and thought that he had seen something. I looked behind him, and a small bull was watching the boy from not thirty yards away. The direction that the boy was looking told me that he had no idea that the small elk was there. The bull was partly hidden by the brush, and it was looking to where he heard the bugling come from. The boy made another long bugle, and that was about all the young bull could take. He broke from cover with blood in his eye and was going to kill an intruder or at the very least run him off his mountain.

My son turned when he heard the elk running. The gun came to my shoulder as it had done so very many times, in exactly the right position, with the safety off and my finger on the trigger. It had barely taken five steps when my reliable old 45-70 government rifle barked. The bull skidded downhill on his chest and stopped still barely three feet from my boy. It usually took quite a bit to get me excited, but I was shaking inside and out, and it sure wasn't from the cold.

My young son and I both learned something that morning. He learned that to be a live breathing hunter, he was going to need eyes in the back of his head. I learned once again how very much I loved my son."

Matt was silent as the tears welled up in the old man's eyes. He turned to face the darkness and walked to his tent, needing some time to be alone.

Matt sat near the fire, feeding it small pieces of wood and bark that lay on the ground. He took a small drink from Wil's jug and sat back down on his oak stump. The warmth of the campfire felt good to him, and for a moment, he let his thoughts get away from him, like a small bird let loose from his hand.

Many of his years as a young man had been relegated to the very back of his memory, and only rarely did he let them come out. He thought of times when he was a small boy. His father drank himself to near oblivion each night, and like so many cowards, he looked for someone to beat on. Most times it was his wife, and she taunted him until he hit her and knocked her to the floor. His mother drank nearly as much whiskey as his father. At other times, he chased her from room to room with his revolver, trying his best to get a shot at her. He eventually passed out, and she retrieved the gun to hide it from him again. The pistol shots sometimes came through the floor of Matt's bedroom, and he moved to a safer place to pass the night.

Matt always looked forward to Christmas, even though he had seen few that were worth remembering. There was always a decorated tree and presents for him to open. He got excited, waiting for the big moment, but as the day wore on and it got closer to the time to open the gifts, his father always got too drunk to participate. The day always ended in a shouting match.

Other times, he was the target of his fathers wrath in a more serious way. When his fury got more out of control, Matt ran from the house with his father right behind him. He headed for the swamp, and his father yelled and cursed in his drunken fog. If that didn't work, he tried to run over him with the car as he crossed the streets. The next day the old man had no memory of it at all. At that time in his life, he felt no love for anyone, and he felt that no one loved him. He spent nearly all of his waking hours on his school work and excelled in all of his classes. It was his only means of escape.

He checked out many books from the library, and that gave him a first class ticket to anywhere he wanted to go. He hunted the African plains with Jack O'Connor and stalked the giant elk of Colorado with Fred Bear, using only a straight bow. He saw places that no other kid in the world had seen. He met all the great presidents and the Babe himself, all in the library.

At other times, he turned on his old vacuum tube radio and listened as the Lone Ranger rounded up the bad guys, and Fibber McGee and Molly made him laugh so hard that he forgot where he was until the soap commercials came on. Then his favorite story teller came on and tried to sell Buster Brown shoes.

"I'm Buster Brown. I live in a shoe. Here's my dog Tyke. He lives here, too." Andy Divine said, "Plunk your magic twanger Froggie."

Froggie jumped out of a shoe box and said, "Hiya, kids. Hiya. Hiya."

On some nights when the air was right, he heard stations from very far away, and that set him off dreaming again. These were magical moments for young Matt, and he never forgot those many nights he hid in his bedroom and basked in the yellow-orange glow of the old Zenith radio.

As he grew older, he was determined to do all of the things that let him escape reality as a child. He made a trip to Michigan when he turned eighteen to meet the famous archer that had written so many books and was one of his heroes. The words of encouragement from this man carried him through his college days and into medical school.

The night air was getting colder. Matt turned up the collar of his coat to block the chill wind. Eventually, the cold got the best of him, and he headed to his tent for the night.

Chapter 4: The Doe

The morning dawned, clear and cold, and the aroma of fresh boiled coffee filled the air. Wil sat on an oak stump and stared into the fire, his hat drawn low over his forehead.

"Are you ready?"

"I'd like to see a big buck sometime."

"Well, if you want to take one home, a buck's fine, but for the meatpole, we should stick to small does and fawns. When Ma cans that venison, it comes out as tender as a mother's.

"I don't really want to take one home, since the wife doesn't like it anyway."

Wil poured them some coffee and sat down again on his stump.

"What's in the pot? My stomach thinks my throat's been cut."

"Grits." Wil laughed. "Want some?"

"Sure. I think I could eat a skunk right now."

Matt wasn't at all sure what grits were, but he was so darned hungry that he was willing to try nearly anything.

Wil took the lid off the pot and poured something onto Matt's plate. Matt stared at the plate. Wil gave him an amused look as if he couldn't quite believe that Matt had never eaten grits.

"You put salt and pepper on 'em and sometimes a little butter. Bread goes pretty good with 'em, too."

Matt reached for the salt and pepper and found a chunk of bread, too. The grits looked like food, and he was awful hungry. He dunked his bread into the grits and stuffed it into his mouth.

"It doesn't have much taste except for the salt and pepper."

He took another bite. He wasn't sure where grits came from. He didn't know if they were vegetable, animal, or mineral. He kept eating just the same. Wil looked at him once in a while and grinned. Was this a test to see how tough Matt was? They kept eating, and when they were through, he told Matt that it was ground up white corn, and he had grown up on the stuff. It made Matt wonder how he had ever gotten this old.

The morning sun climbed a bit higher in the sky, and it was time to head to the woods. They walked quietly down a gravel road. Every so often, they jumped a ruffed grouse, and the whirring sound made Matt jump. They didn't want to do any shooting now and spook the deer. They decided that Matt would crawl up in a big oak tree, and Wil would try to move something into range for him to get a good shot. Matt found a tree with a lot of branches and nearby a small clearing. He got settled in on a high limb. He had been there for a couple hours when he heard something coming through the brush. There was a flicker of antlers, and Matt watched intently. First came a small doe, and right behind her was the biggest buck that he had ever seen. He had a rack that hunters only dream of, and there were points going every which way. His neck was swelled up like a big bull, and he had a lot of gray on his muzzle. The small doe entered the clearing and hesitated for a moment.

Time stood still. The grass of the clearing sparkled as if each blade of grass were decorated with small diamonds. All Matt heard was the delicate sound of the doe's steps as she entered the clearing. The old buck sauntered up next to her, and with his foreleg, slapped her in the rump, as if to say,

"How about it babe?"

Even his smallest movements seemed to take on a regal air as he moved slowly and confidently.

That was about all that Matt could take. Up came the 12 gauge, and he sighted down the barrel. He had the buck dead to rights, and what a trophy he was. Then, Wil's words came to him.

"Does and fawns" he had said.

Matt really didn't want to disappoint Wil, so he dropped the barrel a bit and squeezed the trigger. The doe went down quickly, and the trophy buck was gone before the smoke cleared.

In a couple minutes, Wil appeared in the clearing.

"Did you see him?"

"See what?" Matt said, hoping that he didn't mean that big buck.

"That big one. That was a once in a lifetime trophy. I sure would like to have had a crack at him. I caught a glimpse of him twice, and that rack had to be the biggest I've ever seen."

Well, that cinched it for Matt. Here he was in some damned old oak tree freezing his tail feathers off and in comes the biggest buck on God's green earth. And what did Matt do? He shot the runt, the baby. Was there something gone mushy in his head? Didn't he have any common sense? Wil looked at him with a slight grin and asked him again if he saw him.

"Yup I did, but as I pulled the trigger, the doe jumped up, and the slug hit her instead, but at least we got something for the meat pole. Right?"

"Yup, I guess it must have been fate."

No matter how bad Matt wanted to tell Wil the truth, he figured that he would look bad no matter what he said. If he said that he took the doe to please Wil, it would look like he had no ability to make his own decisions. Why was he so damned intent on pleasing the old man? He was an adult for god's sake and a doctor to boot!

Wil walked over to the doe and saw the entire story in the tracks. He had been at this business far too many years to be fooled.

"Yup." Wil said. "Fate."

They gutted out the doe and saved the liver and heart for supper. There wasn't much to her, so they dragged it back to camp.

They cut up the haunches first and then sliced it into quarter inch slices. From there it went into a brine for curing. In time they hung it all up to dry over a slow fire. The hide was salted and rolled for tanning at home. The tanned deer skin made great mittens and shirts.

By the time they finished with their work, it was getting dark. Wil again was doing the cooking.

"You slice up the liver and heart, but not too thick now, and I'll cut up some onion." Wil said.

In few minutes, Wil had coffee cooking and the liver and heart in the pan along with an onion. He added a little side pork fat and sat and watched it. Soon the pan was sizzling and all sorts of good aromas were hitting Matt. Wil waited to see how long Matt could last. In a half an hour, he announced that the food was ready.

Matt had a hard time eating enough to stay alive back in Minneapolis. Food didn't much appeal to him. Here in their hunting camp it was a much different story. Wil was cooking things that set off wake up alarms inside Matt's head. He was always ready for another mealtime. The supper tasted as good as it had smelled. Back in Minneapolis, people were dining on fat pork chops and sirloins, not knowing what they were missing. The liver was strong flavored but very tender, and the heart was chewy and also full of flavor. Both were fried to a perfect crisp on the outside. Wil sliced off another chunk of hard bread for each of them, and again they ate in silence.

Matt only had one day left to stay in camp. He tried to put it from his mind unsuccessfully. He'd have to play catch up when he got back. There would be a backlog of surgeries. The thing that grated on him the most was the head of the hospital. He was an arrogant twit with scarcely enough brains to zip up his own trousers. Many times he had wanted to walk out at 5:00 p.m. and never look back, but his wife kept urging him to stick with it. He wondered sometimes what would happen if the ready supply of money ever dried up.

After they finished eating and the pans were put away, they sat near the fire, neither of them saying much. Wil reached behind him and pulled out the whiskey jug. He handed it to Matt who winced a bit at the thought and took a swallow from the jug to be polite. It was surprisingly cool to the mouth and had a slightly woody flavor. He handed it back to Wil who seemed to be looking for some sort of a reaction. There was none, and it pleased the old man. He also took a long drink from the jug and set it down between them.

"What was life like when you were a kid up here?"

"Well, it was fun, but darned tough sometimes. We never had any cash money and times were hard for my Pa. We didn't even know that we were poor though, until I got old enough to go to school. We always ate real good and wore homemade clothes. At school, lunch was sometimes a lard and sugar sandwich from an old sugar sack, but it tasted pretty good to me. Some of the other kids were from town and dressed in better clothes than we did, so I guess they thought that they were a little better than us. Didn't matter, though, because we quit school before we got to eighth grade, right before we started noticing how pretty the girls were."

Wil thought in silence for a minute and recalled one of his favorite times of the year.

"Christmas was always special at our house. We would go and cut the very best spruce tree that we could find and bring it home for Ma to trim. She had several small paper stars and shiny things that would spin when we walked by the tree. We popped some corn and strung it on thread with some bright red cranberries, and then Ma would hang it on the tree. The top of the tree was always reserved for special decorations that my pa had made. They held a small candle, and on Christmas Eve, he would light them, and we'd sing some of our favorite Christmas songs. These were happy times for us all. In the early morning we would wake up to find a gift from old St. Nick. It was usually a new pair of woolen mittens and sometimes a peppermint candy cane. Some years, we got a big orange."

Wil's old face clouded a bit, and his voice seemed to falter. He took a deep breath and sat for a minute.

"The timber wolves sure gave us a lot of trouble back then. One bad winter the snow had come early, and most of the deer had left the area or died of slow starvation. With nothing for them to eat, the wolves turned to our livestock. First, it was a young pig, and a couple days later, they took a good bull calf that we were saving for breeding stock. They had the calf nearly eaten by the time we found it. At the time I was about thirteen, and Pa wanted me to help get rid of the wolves. He told me to get on the roof of the barn and wait there with the shotgun loaded full of buckshot. The full moon came up at about 7:00, and I was ready. I remember that it was awful cold out. Pa had staked one of the sheep outside, and it was making a terrible commotion wanting back inside the barn. In a frantic rush, a timber wolf was on it and dragged it to the ground. He had it by the throat, and then the three others joined in. Altogether it took about five seconds, and it was over. The wolves were loudly snarling at each other, trying to decide who'd get to eat first. I took careful aim, and when the old shotgun went off, the flash blinded me for a bit. I reloaded, and when the smoke cleared enough for me to shoot again, I saw that three of the timber wolves were stone dead and that another one was rolling around on the ground. I squeezed the trigger and finished him off.

At forty yards, the heavy buckshot had done its job. We lost another of our sheep, but we gained a welcome eight dollars from the bounty money. It wasn't enough to pay for the lost stock, but it helped quite a bit with money being so scarce and all. Pa was right there as soon as he heard the racket and swore that he had never seen such fine shooting."

Wil smiled a bit as he told the last part.

"Did you have any more trouble with the wolves that year?"

"No, they seemed to dislike the taste of lead." said Wil grinning. "Those were tough times, but we managed because we stuck together. The farm chores were shared by us all. Hard work and plenty of hard laughing was what made us a close family."

Wil became a little more quiet and sat for a while enjoying the campfire. He held the backs of his hands so that the fire would warm them. He had crooked old fingers and his arthritis plagued him severely.

"Time for me to turn in, Matt. I did want to get some more ducks tomorrow. I saw some redheads coming in right before dark this evening. Them and canvasbacks come down late in the year. It'll be a good shoot tomorrow."

"You know, Wil. I don't know if I've ever shot a canvasback."

"They're a good sized duck. You'll have to be quick tomorrow."

Wil turned and headed into his tent. Soon his loud snoring was all that broke the silence of the night. Matt thought for a minute and realized that he had to leave camp by tomorrow night if he were to make it back in time. He had some appointments to keep and patients to heal; although, he figured that fully half of them would heal nicely with a few sugar pills. Again, he wrapped his body around the fire pit, enjoying the show.

He thought back to when he was in tenth grade at school.

His best friend had asked him if he wanted to go hunting for bear, down the far end of Hale Lake, and Matt decided to go. As the morning sky started to lighten, they headed to Hale Lake and got into a flat bottomed cedar boat. They paddled down the mile long lake. Both of them were anxious. When they stepped out onto the shore, they were both shaking. They didn't know if it was from the cold or fear or a combination. Matt was armed with an old Winchester Model 94, 30-30 he had borrowed, and Duane had a 16 gauge with slugs. They put out the bait, a large bucket of rotten fish guts. At that point they expected a bear to come running in headed for suicide.

They sat down on the ground and waited. Pretty soon they heard something coming through the woods headed right for them. Duane leaned over and said that he heard something coming from the other direction too. It was at that moment that they decided that they better sit back to back so nothing could sneak up on them. The sounds took a great leap in volume, and it was at that moment the intrepid hunters decided to head back home where it was a little safer. Looking back on that morning, Matt figured that what they heard were squirrels, bent on getting even with them for their previous merciless attacks.

Chapter 5: Mixed Bag

Morning found Wil and Matt up early, getting ready for the hunt. Wil had whipped together some flapjacks and covered them up nicely with maple syrup and butter. That and coffee made for another unforgettable meal.

The two friends walked slowly down the dike in the darkness listening to the ducks fly over. Each stopped at their accustomed spot and sat down to wait. As daylight came, the ducks moved in by the hundreds. It was like Wil had said, canvasbacks and redheads. These were large ducks, and they seemed a bit harder to kill than geese. Matt shot nearly a half of a box of shells before he got his first canvasback. These were tough erratic fliers, and they really kept him on his toes. The sky was turning orange with the promise of a warm day, and as the sun came up into full view, the action stopped for a while. It seemed as though the whole world was holding its breath. Then it started again, with small flocks of eight or ten, but they seemed never to end.

When they had shot all the ducks that they wanted to clean for one day, they decided to call it quits and sat for a while watching the birds flying in from the north.

Matt's thoughts turned to Minneapolis and the hurried rush that takes over a man's soul. He had come here to recharge his batteries, but it somehow had gotten to be something much deeper. He was sure that meeting Wil was what had made it so different. In the few days that he knew him, he taught, or was trying to teach Matt, patience and perseverance, and it made him a bit happier to be alive.

"I think I'll head back to camp." Wil said. "I got a dozen cans to clean, and I want to trap some muskrats. I've been watching them adding to their feeders all morning, and it seems that there's quite a few this year."

Matt decided that he would go, too, since he had to pack for the trip home. Matt cleaned ducks with Wil for a couple hours and turned to cleaning himself. The warm water felt good on his hands and face, and the smell of the soap made him think of home. He went through his car to make room for a few ducks and geese. There was still plenty of room in the back seat, so he started to put his clothes in. He turned his attention to the trunk to see what he could do to rearrange that mess. The first thing that he saw was his black doctor's bag. He noticed the four bottles of liquor he had brought along for severe emergencies, the kind of circumstance where nothing else would do. He had thought for a moment to give one to Wil, but decided to wait.

He looked around, and Wil was headed back down the long dike with a Duluth pack on his back loaded with traps. Matt thought he'd tag along and see what fur trapping was all about. He caught up with Wil as he made his first set. He put the trap right at the edge of the water on a half submerged log.

"No self respecting muskrat could resist that, Matt."

Matt followed him. Every fifty feet, he set another trap.

"Care to give it a try, Matt?"

"Sure."

Matt found a good log to put into the water and cleared a path to it in the tall brown reeds. He wired the trap to a short log. The set met with the old mans approval, and he grinned.

They continued down the dike until they had come nearly full circle. Back at camp they built up the campfire a little, and Wil put on the coffee. As the two sat there enjoying the day, Matt asked him when he would check the traps. Wil said that they would start in about an hour.

When they headed back down the dike, Wil asked Matt to carry the Duluth pack. At the first trap, it was clear that something had been there, but nothing was in the trap, so Wil reset it, and they continued down the dike.

The next trap hadn't been touched, but the one after that had a large muskrat in it. Wil deftly opened the jaws of the trap and reset it. He threw the rat in the pack, and they continued. By the time they had finished the trapline, they had a total of thirteen muskrats. Matt silently wondered what the next step was and didn't have long to wait to find out. Wil could skin a rat in about ten seconds. The small ones he kept in a pile by the fire, and the others he threw in a pile by the oak tree. The fresh skins were turned inside out and slipped over pine stretching boards to dry. With a strange kind of knife, he scraped all of the fat off the hides. This seemed to take no time, and he arranged them all so as to dry quickly. The rats brought cash money, something Wil always was in need of. Most years, he could count on about eight cents for a prime pelt, but he had heard that the going price might be somewhat higher, possibly as high as fifteen cents.

The darkness jumped on them in a hurry. He hadn't been watching Wil too closely, and when he said that supper was ready, Matt came on the run. Each meal that he made was food fit for a king. He handed Matt a blue enamel plate and a hot biscuit to sop up the thick brown gravy. He was enjoying it far too much to ask what it was. It wasn't until they had finished that Wil told Matt that it was marsh hare, a well known delicacy in France.

Now where did Wil get that? This was muskrat, and Matt knew it. Had he turned into one of those jackpine savages he'd heard about? It was hard telling at that moment, but the transformation had already begun.

Again a full belly was making Matt tired, and again Wil took out the jug of whiskey. He pulled out the cork, and this time, he threw it into the fire. Matt knew what that meant, and he was up to the challenge. He offered Matt first pull, and he swallowed a couple gulps. It was Wil's turn. He tipped the jug up and kept it to his lips for quite a while. When he finished, he sat it down carefully near the fire. Neither man said anything for several minutes.

"Are you leaving tonight, Matt?"

"Yup. I have a long drive ahead of me and really should have left last night. It's nearly three hundred miles back home."

"That's a far piece this time of year. Pass me that jug, Matt. I need something to keep the chill off me."

The jug was passed, and Wil took another large drink. He passed it back and sat watching the fire. After another round or two, the doctor was starting to feel a little fuzzy. He closed his eyes for a moment and sleep overtook him.

Wil sat for a while looking at the now slumbering doctor and thought of times when his son and he had camped in this very place together. *Time had gone by so quickly*, he thought. It seemed to him like just yesterday when he gave the boy his first shotgun. He turned to the day that the boy wanted to join the Navy. The old man hadn't wanted the boy to go, but he knew that there was no sense in telling him no. He would have been eighteen soon, anyway, and he really wanted to enlist. He was a determined boy, and when he got something in his head, it was time to move back a step or two.

After he enlisted, he was sent to some far off place for boot camp. Wil didn't hear from him for quite some time, and then a letter came that said he was well and that they fed him pretty good. There was a lot to learn, but he was managing. He said that they tested him to see what he would be best at and were sending him to Naval Gunnery School. That suited the boy fine since he had been around guns for most of his life. He closed sending his love. He had also included a ten dollar bill. Wil hadn't seen one of those in quite a while, so he chose to save it for the boy. He'd need it when he came back home. There was an old Prince Albert tobacco can on the table that Wil used for storing his fish hooks, and Wil placed the money in it and put it up on the fireplace mantel.

The boy wrote about once a month, and when the letters came, Wil read them to his wife. She never had learned to read very well. At the end of each letter, they got down the Prince Albert can and put in ten dollars.

As time went by, the boy was sent out to sea duty. His letters sounded like he was enjoying the Navy and had completed the gunnery school at the top of his class. He said that they had planes tow targets past them, and he never missed. He also said that the ocean was as blue as Ma's eyes, and that made her cry.

Quite a bit of time went by until they heard from him again. This time he said that he was in Hawaii and told about how beautiful it was. He also said that he had tasted fresh pineapple for the first time and how sweet it was. There was always a ten dollar bill enclosed, and it always went into the Prince Albert can.

One evening, as they sat eating their supper, they heard a soft knock on the cabin door. Wil opened it, and there stood a man all dressed in white. It took a moment for Wil to realize that it was that scrawny kid of his, all grown up. That smile of his gave him away, and he grabbed for his pa and gave him a fierce hug. He looked over his pa's shoulder, and when Ma saw him, she gave out a shriek that would have woke the dead. She was crying and laughing all at the same time. It had been nearly two years. It took quite some time for all their voices to calm down, but they wound up at the kitchen table like old times. Ma lit another oil lantern, and the house took on a cheery glow. The boy was home.

Father and son spent a lot of time together trying hard to erase all of those days apart. They fished and worked in the hillside garden together, and the boy told sea stories to his pa. Evenings they talked until their eyes couldn't stay open any longer.

The days seemed to go by altogether too fast, and one night at supper, the boy announced that he had to leave again soon. He was due back in Hawaii the following Monday. He had a couple days left, and they were spent talking and enjoying their time together. His ma cooked all of the boy's favorite dishes, and he seemed to gain a couple pounds in the week he was home.

The next morning, Ma cooked some ham and eggs for breakfast, and the boy ate a good meal. He left to go to his room and came back again all dressed in white with two service ribbons on his uniform. He sure looked good, and his shoes shined brightly. It came time to say goodbye, and he put his arms around his pa and held him tightly for a while. He handed him three crisp twenty dollar bills. He turned to his ma and saw the tears running slowly down her cheeks. He held her tenderly as if she would break, and it seemed that he didn't want to let her go. Then, it was time to leave. He opened the door and walked out into the bright sunshine. He had a long slow walk to the bus station in town, but it gave him time to gather himself together.

Wil and his wife stood at the cabin door, eyes clouded with tears, and watched their only son walk down the dusty road. Wil took the money and once again put it in the can.

In a month or so, they got another letter from the boy with another ten dollars inside. He said that he was doing very well and was looking forward to another visit in a year. He also said that he had met a girl, and her name was June. They both smiled.

One day in early winter, Wil picked up a new battery for the radio at the general store. They hooked it up, and for a while it wasn't sure whether or not it wanted to work. Through the static they heard their President speaking. The radio faded in and out for a while. He said something about a cowardly raid on Pearl Harbor and named some ships that were sunk. It was hard to make out what he said, but they both knew that it was something bad. It was December of 1941.

The next day they walked to the general store. There were a lot of people out front, and from what Wil could hear, America was at war with Japan. They left for home without saying a word.

Supper that night was quiet, not the usual chatter. They were seriously worried about their boy and couldn't get the old radio to work at all.

The next few days were tense for them both. They were eating supper when they heard a car pull into the pine covered yard. Then, there was a knock on the door. A man in white was standing there with his hat in his hand, and they knew right away what he had to say. Before the man could speak a word, Ma had tears streaming down her face.

A couple days later, they got another letter from the boy. He said that he was going to get married to June next week before he left for sea duty. He said that he knew that June would fit right in with the rest of the family and how she had such a pretty smile. There was the usual ten dollars enclosed. Through his tear filled eyes, Wil found the Prince Albert can and placed the money inside.

Chapter 6: The Harvest

Morning came, and eventually Matt awoke. He squinted across the fire, and Wil handed him a cup of coffee.

"Damn! I feel like I been run over by a truck."

"Time to go and check the traps pretty soon. I didn't have the heart to wake you last night. You were out pretty early and snoring hard. I thought that the whiskey might have gotten to you, but maybe you were just tired."

Matt looked at him and for a moment thought to defend his falling asleep, but he knew that he had messed up and should have been back in Minneapolis by now. His cup of coffee burned his hand, so he set it on a rock to cool.

"You know, Wil, I should be in the operating room right now. I hate to think what my boss might be saying."

Wil grinned at him and sipped his coffee.

"I can imagine what my wife is thinking. She probably figures that I shot myself."

Wil continued to sip his coffee.

"I suppose you're pretty hungry." said Wil.

"Maybe I better wait a while for that."

Matt couldn't bring himself to take anything much stronger than coffee. His head felt like he'd had a close call with ether. That fire water was extremely potent, and somewhere during the night, the old man had finished what was left.

The walk to the dike seemed a little further than usual, and it took Matt a while to get his legs under him.

The first trap had another muskrat in it, and that brought a smile to Wil's face. The old man let Matt make the sets, and in a couple hours, he could reset the traps quite well. Some of them were iced over, so they had to be moved a bit. The fall sunshine was bright, but the air was cold, and Matt's hands were stiff from being in the icy water. The old man saw him having trouble setting one trap and took it from him. Wil had it reset in a moment, and they walked on nearing their camp again. They had sixteen rats, and that was enough to keep Wil happy. By the time they had completed the loop, it was nearly noon. After a donut and a cup of coffee, they both headed into their canvas tents to take a nap. Matt left the large flap of the tent open and laid down in the fall sunshine. He was asleep in a short time.

Wil, on the other hand, spent his time sitting and thinking. The combination of Matt's good company and his advanced years made him think of days gone by. He thought of a time when he was a young man. He and his beloved wife had only been married a few years. He was a handsome tall man with a coal black beard and long black hair. His wife was a small woman with beautiful blue eyes and blonde hair.

They had moved to southern Minnesota to try farming, and the good Lord had blessed their marriage with twin boys. These were happy times for Wil. The children were cheerful and never lacked for attention. Wil brought them something from town each time he went. They got to know that when Dad came into the house, they should look into his shirt pocket. A gum ball or some green spearmint leaf candies were always popular. They made Wil's eye sparkle each time he saw them. The boys were always together, and when they reached their third birthday, they kept their mother quite busy just keeping them out of trouble.

Wil had a sixty acre farm, and it took most of his daylight hours to make it pay. He was no stranger to hard work, and now fall was in the air, and it was harvest time. Threshing season was like payday for a farmer. The grain was ready for harvest, and a threshing team was hired to come in and process the grain. They took a quarter of the grain for their efforts, and it seemed like a lot sometimes, but Wil didn't have to buy the machinery. The threshing was usually done in an open field. They brought in the machine and horses early in the morning. By the time that the dew was off the fields, they were ready to get to work. Four horses were hitched to a large center spindle and continued going around in a circle. The power was transferred to the threshing machine by a very long belt. The thresher knocked off the grain and sent the chaff up through a large pipe by a fan. The grain was bagged and stacked. Wagons made continuous trips from field to thresher to the barns for storage. It took a crew of at least twelve men to make it all work.

As noon approached, the women brought out what they had been cooking, and the hired hands ate a good hot meal. It was usually meat, potatoes, and bread, and this was part of their pay. There was always lots of hot coffee. The children were there at that time, and everyone let them go and have fun, as long as they stayed away from the horses. The threshing machine was looked over, and some of the moving parts were oiled to get ready for the rest of the days work. There was a small door on the back side where you could get at the knives that chopped the chaff before it went up into the fan to be blown into a pile. It had a latch that locked when you slammed it shut.

All the men were fed and ready to get back to work. The boss started the team moving again, and the lead man put the threshing machine in gear. The fan whirred, and the sickle bars ran back and forth on the machine. Wil heard a slight noise and looked up in time to see pieces of clothing and blood come out with the chaff. He looked around for his wife, and she looked at Wil. The kids weren't around. The boss stopped the horses, and the machine quieted down. Ma screamed, and Wil stood there with his arms around her. They both knew what had happened. The boys had entered the knife section that was left open, and the wind had blown the door shut behind them. They were always together, always.

Their worst fears were confirmed when the threshing boss opened up the machine. There wasn't much left in there, so he started the machine again and blew the section clear with a load of chaff. One of the neighbors rode to town and got the sheriff and a preacher. Everyone prayed, and the sheriff lit the chaff pile on fire. The smoke from the pile of chaff carried for several miles. Wil and Ma never did get over that.

Wil's eyes clouded a bit when he remembered his kids. He couldn't figure how one family could have such trouble. The good Lord had given them three wonderful kids and then taken them back. He wondered silently why. There was an almost audible slamming of the old memory box lid as he closed his eyes.

Matt came out and closed up his tent. He walked over to the fire and threw on a couple pieces of oak. He warmed the coffee and poured them each a cup.

"Did you get a nap, Wil?"

"No. I was too darned busy thinking. When it gets quiet at times, I start thinking about my family."

"How big a family did you and your wife have?"

"We had the three boys, but in Gods time, they all died. So now it's the old woman and me. Somehow, I had figured that it would be a lot different than this."

Matt was filled with questions, but he knew that he should ask no more. Wil had a pained look on his face, but he tried to smile.

"Let's drink this coffee and get to work." Wil said.

Matt drank his in silence, not wanting to interrupt the old mans thoughts. In a couple gulps, Wil was done and standing there waiting to run the trapline. Wil usually didn't have much to say when they were walking, but today he had a few words saved up.

"When are you heading back to Minneapolis?"

"Yesterday." he said, and they both laughed. "I guess I should be home by now, but I can't leave here. I feel like I have found that one thing that a man looks for all of his life. It's a feeling of being satisfied with where I am. I never had that before. I was always looking over the next hill. My uncle said that I had wanderlust."

"I guess that I found my spot years ago because I was born there on the river. It's been my home for a lot of years. I doubt that I could pry the old woman from there anyway. There's a lot of memories in our old shack."

The warm afternoon sun had gotten the muskrats really moving. They must have been expecting a really bad winter. Their feeders were big this year, and the pelts were extra thick, too. That and the woolie bear caterpillars having a thick coat, usually meant that they were in for a bad one. Some don't put much stock in such things, but

Wil did, and with good reason.

By the time they had made their rounds, it was dark again, and there were hides to be stretched. The men worked well together, and the job was done in a couple hours. Matt noticed that Wil hadn't kept any rats for dinner, and he was somewhat relieved by that.

"What's for supper tonight, Wil?" Matt asked.

He laughed a gravelly roar, and it surprised Matt a bit.

"What do you think this is, a hotel?"

They both laughed.

"I guess I could show you what a great cook I am." he said kind of sheepishly.

He went over to his car, and in the trunk, he found a can of pork and beans. He rustled up some smoked sausage and a few potatoes. There was still a bit of pork fat in the pan, so he made some fried potatoes and as they were getting done, he threw in some large chunks of smoked sausage. It was starting to smell pretty darned good. A little breeze came through the camp and stirred up the fire. Ashes flew into the pan, but it didn't seem to matter to either of them. He opened the can of beans and set it close to the fire.

Soon the beans were bubbling away, and the meal was complete. He took the two blue enameled pans and filled one heaping full with his creations and handed it to Wil, along with a cup of steaming hot coffee. Wil brought out a couple soda biscuits and some butter. He handed one to Matt, and the feast got under way. They both ate like they hadn't eaten for weeks.

Matt took the dishes down to the stream and washed them well, using sand to scrub out the burned parts. He thought for a moment about Wil and how he had turned out to be a very interesting man and in some regards kind of a mystery. He never seemed to offer much in the way of conversation, but when asked anything, he was willing to share his insight. He thought of that jug of whiskey and wondered if the old man had made it himself, or did he buy it with his short supply of cash. A whiskey still surely was illegal, but everyone knew that there were a lot of them in the back woods. It was too far into the back country for the law to go nosing about, and sometimes they never got home again if they did. Matt thought about the bottle that he had brought from home, a gift from a doctor friend. It was Courvassier cognac. This was an expensive gift, and Matt had saved it. Since the other jug was gone, he looked in the trunk and retrieved it. He carried it back to the campfire.

"Now what did you find?" asked Wil.

"Well, I got this bottle of cognac from an old friend in Minneapolis a couple years ago, and I've been saving it for a special occasion. I think if I looked real hard, I'd find a couple other bottles in there too. I guess being here on the Roseau is good enough reason to open one up." said Matt.

He held it up to the firelight and examined it closely. He broke the paper seal and handed it to Wil.

"Don't believe that I ever had anything like this before!"

"Well, as far as I can remember, it's made in France and costs a lot of money. That's all I know about it."

Wil wiped his mouth with the back of his sleeve and put the amber bottle to his lips. He took a small drink and held it in his mouth for a bit before swallowing. He took a larger drink and passed it back to Matt.

"Mighty fine!"

Matt raised the bottle and took some for himself. It had a warm feel all the way down his throat and into his belly.

"It is indeed," said Matt agreeing with the old man.

After a couple more hours of small talk, they had emptied the bottle. The fire was starting to die down a bit, and there was a warm fall wind out of the south. Matt stretched out on the bare ground near the fire, like he did most nights, and was out in short order. The old man was left alone again with his thoughts of family, places, and times past.

Chapter 7: Bustikogan

In his many years living on the Bigfork River, Wil heard several stories of an Indian Chief named Bustikogan. Many stories were told of the man, but mostly, he was known as being a great leader of his people. As with most tales, reality wasn't as interesting as the stories people told. Bustikogan traveled northern Minnesota visiting the logging camps. He was welcomed wherever he went. He had a pleasant manner and was always ready to help a friend. He was noted mostly for his wide smile and wrinkled face. He had a knowledge of many things from the white's world. Over his numerous years on the river, Wil eventually became close friends with him.

One winter when the snows had come early, Wil and his wife were eating supper by the light of the old kerosene lamp. Neither said much, and when they heard footsteps crunching in the snow, they looked at each other, puzzled. Wil was up and to the door in a stride or two. As he opened it, he saw the shape of a man, mostly covered with blankets and frost. It was Chief Busti. On this night it was at least thirty below zero. Wil welcomed the old friend into his home and gave him a chair near the fireplace. The old chief still had his usual smile, but his face was thin and drawn. The game had been hit hard by the winter, and hunting was tough for everyone. He had lost a lot of weight and had a terrible cough. Wil found him a plate, and Ma filled it with potatoes and beans. The Indian ate noisily, and Wil couldn't help but think that he hadn't seen food in quite some time. Then, he drank a large cup of coffee.

After Busti was fed and warmed, the conversation turned to his people. It seems that the pox had killed most of his band near the Big White Oak. His two sons and his wife had died, and there were only a few people left there. He had to leave the area and find food for himself as all the others did. It was a serious situation, and Busti called on his old friend to help him until spring. Wil figured that he could keep Busti occupied until he could get back on his feet. The logging camps had turned him away, and old Busti was having a hard time. He didn't like the camps anyway. Every time he went there to work, he got lice from the lumberjacks.

Busti was a lean and tough man from his life in the north of Minnesota. His hands were large, and his fingernails were clean and trimmed neatly. Around his waist he carried a small deerskin bag and on the opposite side a sheathed knife. Around his neck he wore a crucifix on a piece of rawhide. His hair was quite long, but was braided neatly. He was a tough looking man but once you got to know him, you had a friend for life.

Wil had barn repairs to do, and there were the daily chores that could be better done by two. Ma could throw a couple extra potatoes in the pot, and it wouldn't take much to keep him fed. It might take a while, but Ma thought she could fatten him up some.

Busti was given a spot on the floor near the fireplace, and it seemed to suit him well. Ma gave him several heavy wool blankets to sleep on. Such hospitality hadn't been known by this man too often. Now his smile was back, and Wil was glad to have a man to talk to.

Most whites thought of their Indian neighbors as thieves and robbers, and some were, but it was the same for the world of the whites. Some were good, and some were bad, but you always remember the bad. Busti had locked horns with the young bucks many times. They stole things to say that they had and to show their friends that they could. It was like counting coup. He had many friends among the whites, and he didn't want them dishonored. He was still chief and a respected man. He could remember a time when there were no white men in these parts. He knew that it was the whites that had brought the pox to his people, and it brought him great sadness to think of how many had died.

The big red pines had brought the whites here, and the iron mines had kept them when the logs were all but gone. Now, the rails cut deeply through the land and carried the timber and iron ore to far off places. The land was changing rapidly, and Busti couldn't keep up with it.

Morning always found Wil stirring early. The fire went out during the night as it always did. He flung both doors wide open and commenced to setting a fresh fire. Busti rolled over and looked at him as if he had gone mad for sure. The cold wind moved through the house like a kiss of death. Wil always said that it was easier to heat fresh air than stale and couldn't be convinced otherwise. Within the time it took for the flames to start, Wil had shut the wind out and was working on a fire for the cookstove. Fresh coffee was always a priority to him. He turned to look at Busti and found him sitting as close to the hearth as he could get without setting his buckskins on fire.

In time, the old woman came out with her gray hair all braided and a smile on her face. She always started each day by kissing Wil on the cheek. Their love for each other had stayed strong for many years and through several hard times and in her waning years. She was still pretty to Wil.

Busti sat down at the table and turned his coffee cup right side up. He, too, liked coffee, but he used a terrible amount of sugar with each cup. Sugar was expensive, and Wil started to say something to Busti and changed his mind.

The days work began in the barn. A couple of the stanchions were worn out, and Wil needed to build new ones. Busti had no idea what a stanchion was or how they worked, so Wil put him to work shoveling manure. Busti understood the job, but he refused to do it. He was, after all, a chief and would not do such work. Wil understood and gave him a job splitting wood. The Indian thought this to be more to his liking and attacked the large woodpile with enthusiasm. They both worked in silence until Wil said that it was about time for lunch. Busti looked at him and said that he had already eaten in the morning. He didn't figure that he should eat again until the next day. Wil almost had to drag the man to the table, but in a few days, Busti was looking forward to meal times as much as Wil. He was starting to put on weight.

Wil had a hog that he had been fattening up for butchering, and Ma and he figured that it was a good day to do it. She started by boiling water, and lots of it. Busti had butchered many animals in his life, but never the way that he was seeing. He couldn't figure out why all the water was boiling. Wil told him that he would cut the animals throat and bleed him out good. They went out to the pen, and Busti hopped the fence and stood by the pig. He had a handful of grain, and the pig ate it hungrily. It seemed like he was trying to make friends with the pig, and Wil decided to watch for a bit. Busti reached down and scratched the pigs head. With his other hand, he reached over the top of the pig with his knife, and in a flash of time, he had cut the pigs throat, and its blood was flowing out onto the ground. The pig still stood there having his head scratched, not knowing that he was almost dead. The knife was so sharp that he never felt it sever his throat. Within ten seconds, the pig tipped over and died without a struggle. Wil had never seen such a humane death. The two hundred pound hog never felt a thing. They lifted the hog by its legs and dropped it into the boiling water for a minute so that it could be scraped clean. After the gutting, they hung the huge animal in the root cellar to cure for a couple days. Ma was ready and had done this job many times. There was headcheese to be made and meat to cut. When all was done, there was sausage to be made and bacon to be cured. The hams were brined and hung in the smokehouse. That evening Ma fried up fresh sweetbreads and onions, one of Wil's favorite meals.

Busti was still the chief of his people and as such held a high position in the Indian community. Word had come to him that there was a message from Washington for him at the general store. The next day, he and Wil walked down to get it. Busti couldn't read, so Wil read it to him aloud. It seemed that one of Minnesota's senators wanted Busti to come and tell about how the pox had killed so many of his people on the Big White Oak. Enclosed was a money draft for two hundred dollars and train tickets there and back. He was expected on February 27th to speak to the United States Senate. There were papers that told of which hotel he would stay at, and who his senate aid would be. It appeared that all was taken care of for him, even his meals. Busti nodded his head in approval and said that he would do this for his people. In five days, he would get on the train in Deer

River to go to Washington.

The trip to town took a bit longer than he thought it would, and by the time that he got on the train to Washington, he was already two days behind schedule. The trip was very interesting to him, but there were few people who talked to him. His appearance was a bit different from most of the passengers. He wore moccasins and beaded buckskin clothes. His hair was greased down and braided. He was certainly a distinctive looking man, but not like the rest of the people on the train.

He rode along in silence, seeing things and places that he had not even heard of. There were great lakes and rivers that you couldn't even see across. There were many black men and several women that wore strange looking hats. He sat in silence absorbing all he could, to tell his numerous friends when he got back.

Finally, after many hours the train arrived in Washington, and the senate aide was there waiting to escort him. Their conversation was brief, and Busti was escorted to the White House to speak. He was on time, but just barely. As he approached the big room, he was starting to feel a bit apprehensive. The senators all made him feel welcome, and the conversation was informal. They were truly interested in what he had to say and told him that they appreciated him coming from so far away to speak to them.

The senators in turn welcomed him and asked him to give his thoughts on the death of so many of his people. Then, it was his turn to speak, but instead of speaking from his chair, he arose to his full height and walked up to the senators' area and took the podium. The senators looked from one to another and didn't say anything.

Chief Bustikogan looked at each man in the room in turn and commenced his oration.

"I am Bustikogan, Chief of the White Oak Band of Chippewa in the land of Minnesota. We have lived in peace with our brothers, the whites, for a very long time. We traded for furs and other goods.

As last winter came to our village, we had many visitors. The women traded for many blankets and steel pots. These men who came to our camp were friends we had known for a very long time.

Some took our women as wives. Both our tribes were made strong.

As the winter became hard, our children started coughing and had bad fever. We took them into our sweat lodges, and it did not help. Our Holy Man held them one by one as they died in his arms. Then the sickness took the old men and women. Our village was dying. When we were down to just a few men, we each went a different direction from the village. The ones left, threw everything we owned into a huge fire and then went into the big pines.

My two young boys and my wife were taken by the sickness. We think it was from the whites that came to our camp. Some of them died, too."

Busti continued for nearly an hour. Then, with a brief wave of his arm, he said, "Thank you for calling me to your council. You have done me a great honor. Mi Gwitch."

Busti left the room feeling like the very important man he was.

The senate aide took him to his hotel and got him settled into his room. He told Busti that he would be back in two hours to take him on a tour of Washington and then to dinner. He was quite pleased with this aide, and they saw many things that he had heard about.

That evening, Busti was taken to his room and shown how everything worked. The room was brightly lit with gas lights, and there was even an indoor bathroom. He looked at the large bed and thought that he would rather sleep on the floor. He took some blankets off the bed and made up a spot near the window. He was tired from his long trip and needed sleep badly. He blew out the gas lamps and settled down on the floor. In a very few minutes, he was asleep.

The next morning, the senate aide went to the desk of the hotel and asked if Busti had been there yet. They hadn't seen him, and there was no answer when he knocked on his door. He walked around for quite some time and still never found him. In the afternoon, the aide came back and looked for Busti again. There was still no answer at his door, so he asked the hotel detective to open it. As the door opened, the smell of gas nearly knocked them over. Putting a cloth over his face, the detective ran in and opened the window and turned off the gas valves. In a short time they were able to get back into the room, and there lay the great Chief Bustikogan, dead from the coal gas lamps. It was a terrible blow to the people of the Big White Oak, and many tales were told of Busti's bravery and leadership. The Great White Father had even presented him with a gold inlaid rifle. It was buried along with him in the land he loved, overlooking the Mississippi River on the Big White Oak.

Wil's thoughts once again came back to the here and now. There was work to do tomorrow, and they still had to get a couple more deer. He looked into the night sky, enjoying the stars and the warm breeze. It would be a good day to cut venison tomorrow. He stretched and walked into his tent.

Chapter 8: The Two-Man Saw

Morning came with a brilliant red sunrise, and the lake was once again filled with ducks and geese. Matt was a little harder to wake this morning. The night's warm breezes were perfect for sleeping, and he made the most of it. By the time he got up, it was daylight. Wil had already begun his walk out to their shooting blind, and Matt hurried to catch up with him.

"Trying to keep all the birds to yourself, Wil?"

"I figured that the soft city life had gotten the best of you. I thought you were heading back to Minneapolis."

"Not yet. I suppose they're starting to wonder what I'm up to, though. I did the very same thing a couple years ago and forgot to come home for nearly a week. The wife gets a little put out, but she knows how I am."

Just then, Wil crouched a bit and brought his shotgun to his shoulder. Matt turned to see what he was aiming at and saw a big Sandhill crane heading right at them. Wil pulled back the hammer and waited for what seemed to be minutes. Matt was peering through the tall canes and saw the whole show. The crane saw Wil and was trying to gain altitude, but all too late as the charge of 12 gauge, number twos, hit him full. The great bird crumpled and hit the water in front of Matt. He had never seen such a sight in his life. He waded out to retrieve Wil's bird and held it high for the old man to see.

The ducks and geese weren't as cooperative that morning. They had all left the lake on the other side, so shooting was sparse. After a couple hours, Wil decided that their time could be used better back at camp. If they were going to stay very much longer, they had to put up some more firewood too. Wil had found a two man saw at the camp last year, and when he left, he had covered it with grease and hung it on the back of a large popple tree.

After the crane and the ducks were cleaned and put away, they got to work cutting wood. There was a big red oak tree nearby that had seen its share of lightning strikes over the years and appeared to be good camp wood. The two advanced on their intended target and decided where to drop the giant. Wil sized it up, and they started to move the saw. Matt pulled, and then Wil pulled. Then Matt pulled, and Wil pulled, or at least, that's how it was supposed to work. They were each expected to pull hard as the saw cut deeply into the tree. It appeared as if Wil was pulling and pushing Matt around like a rag doll. So back and forth they went until, finally, in exasperation, Wil stopped dead and looked Matt straight in the eye.

"Dammit, boy. If you can't pull, at least lift your feet."

Matt looked at him sheepishly, then he started to laugh. Wil joined in the laughing, and in a short time, Matt's embarrassment faded some, but not much. There were so very many things that Matt had never done before and running a two-man saw happened to be one of them. He was determined to do his share of the work and went at it with renewed enthusiasm.

In time, the oak tree was turned into neat piles of firewood. It looked like enough for most of the winter. While hard work was nothing new for Wil, for Matt it was a rare experience. He sat on a stump examining his newly acquired blisters. Matt looked over at Wil and thought about his new hunting partner. He had made a lot of acquaintances but darned few friends.

As the day moved on toward afternoon, the sky turned a steely gray. Wil mentioned that he still had to get a couple more deer, so the plan was set for the evening. This time Wil stood near a clearing, and Matt tried to push something in toward him. Matt walked down the road a short distance and cut to the right, near a low spot covered mostly with water and ice. As he went around the water, he heard something ahead of him and to his left. He changed his course a bit to the left and continued forward toward Wil. He moved very slowly and cautiously. This time he heard a different sound. It was a kind of rattling sound like antlers on brush. The sound continued off to his left, so Matt cut again a bit further to his left to head whatever it was toward the old man. This cat and mouse game continued for a while, and Matt caught a glimpse every once in a while of antler. He still held the memory of that big buck he had let go. Matt found where the animal left the water and was puzzled some by what he saw. It looked like cow tracks, and it appeared to be several animals headed right for Wil.

Then Wil's rifle discharged, and the whole world came to life. There was a loud crashing right in front of Matt, and he saw what appeared to be the biggest animals in the world coming right toward him. Matt brought his shotgun to his shoulder and fired at the biggest one. They all turned again and headed off toward the swamp. After a short while of trying to catch his breath, Wil walked up to him.

"Did you get one?"

"I took a crack at the biggest one, but I think that I missed. That's the first time I've even seen a caribou." said Matt. "Did you get one?"

"I shot a really nice one. Now we have a lot of work to do. There's been caribou around here for a long time, but there's not many left. I thought that they had all moved north, back into Canada."

The hunters had a lot of meat to cut and cure. The following three days were solid work for them. The meat was moved to the camp, a quarter at a time. Larger racks were built for curing the meat, and the hide was again salted and rolled for future use or selling. The cooler weather kept the meat from spoiling, but there was still a sense of urgency. The two men were up at daylight and worked deep into the night by firelight. Little time was taken for eating or talking until the last of the caribou meat was hung on the wooden racks. A large pile of bones and scraps was built up quite a distance from the tents.

Matt looked around on the third day and reached into the car for a new jug. Most of the work had been done, and now it was time to take a deep breath and relax a bit.

The sun was setting, and it felt warm on the old mans face. The winter would be a little easier this year. With a good supply of meat and some left over to sell, he and the old woman would be fine. Might even be some money left over for her sewing and some new shoes.

He looked over at Matt and had to grin a bit. When he first met the doc, he was clean shaven and dressed in the appropriate clothes for a city hunter, boots and all. Now it was a different story altogether. Matt had the start of a pretty good beard, and his hair hadn't been combed for days. His coat was covered with animal hair, blood, and grease. Those expensive pants were torn and tattered and full of grease. His hands, that were once the hands of a talented surgeon, now looked like he hadn't seen water since the great flood. He smelled badly, and Wil thought it a bit strange that Matt didn't recognize it.

After the two had passed the jug around a couple times, the old man walked over with a grin and handed Matt a piece of a broken mirror.

"Take a look."

Matt moved toward the fire a bit and held up the mirror so he could see better. At first, it seemed that he was having trouble seeing, but within a few seconds he had a kind of proud look on his face. There, looking back at him in the mirror, was the man that he had always wanted to be. There was now a kind of a hard look on his face that soap and water would never wash away. Matt had changed, and he liked what he saw. The jack pine savage, that he had always yearned to be, was emerging and the city doctor was fading into the past.

Wil took back the piece of mirror and placed it deep in his ruck sack. When his hand reappeared, it contained a large piece of homemade lye soap. Matt grinned a bit and took the hint. He went to his tent and took off the old rags. He stripped down to nothing but skin and walked calmly to the edge of the lake. He stood there for a while, and then he calmly walked into the freezing water up to his chest. He made a terrible blood curdling howl and commenced to washing layer after layer of grime from his body. Wil thought for a while that Matt was singing, as he scrubbed. He cleaned every inch of himself and then walked out of the lake and back to the tent. After a few minutes Matt came out wearing clean clothes. He still looked a bit rough around the edges. His hair was slicked down, and there was a real sparkle to his eyes. He appeared to be a new man.

Matt walked over to the old man and handed him the bar of soap. Wil grinned and thought of doing the same routine, but common sense told him to be a bit more cautious. He heated water in the big pot and retired to his tent to bathe, and put on fresh clothes. When he came out of the tent, the campfire was building, and they warmed themselves with flames, stories, and drink.

"I didn't think that you could survive a dunk in water that cold." said Wil.

"After I got in, I wasn't a bit sure I would either. I was kind of hoping for a quick heart attack." Matt said, and they both laughed.

The fire was doing what it was supposed to do, and the men were soon warmed through. They seemed like they had a lot to say, but neither spoke for quite some time. When things had settled down in camp a bit, Wil put his finger to his lips and pointed off into the dark. He was looking intently at the bone pile with eyes that sparkled like black diamonds. Matt stared hard but couldn't see anything. As his eyes became a bit more accustomed to the dark, he saw a quick flicker of yellow eyes.

"Wolves," whispered Wil.

They sat there watching as a pair of light colored wolves took turns snatching chunks of meat and bone. With each quick grab, they stepped back into the darkness and disappeared. They were absolutely silent. Wil thought for a moment about how much a pair of wolf hides would bring in bounty and decided that he had done enough killing for this trip. They watched in silence until the wolves had eaten their fill and left.

"Ever seen wolves that close before?" Matt asked.

"In this part of the country, we're in a constant battle with them critters. They take what's ours, and we try to stop them. It's a war to see which of us is going to survive the winters. So far we're winning."

The two sat for a while watching the fire. It seemed that the longer they knew each other, the less they needed to talk.

"What kind of work is there up here in the winter?"

"There's logging, but there's not much of that left anymore. All the big camps have closed. We used to work as long as there was snow on the ground. The river pigs stayed on until all the logs were pushed to the mills. Then, it was back to our homes again until it snowed."

Chapter 9: The Logging Camps

Wil stared into the fire and told Matt about his youth when he cut the big pines.

"Many years back, I heard from some of my friends that the Diamond T. Logging Camp was looking for sawyers, so I headed down river to see the foreman. My light canoe made a short trip of the twelve miles. The camp was close to the Little Rose waterfall. It had snowed some, but not enough to work yet.

I found the foreman in the blacksmith's shop and hit him up for a job. He was a small man with extraordinarily huge hands. My large fingers looked small in his grip. The foreman wore a black knit hat and a leather vest. He was an altogether mean looking man. There was no doubt that he fought his way to his position in the camp.

The first thing he did was to shake hands with me, not to be friendly, but to see if I had calluses or the soft hands of a gambler. Gamblers weren't allowed in the camps because they were nothing but trouble. Next, he asked what other camps I had worked. There was no sense in trying to fool the foreman. He knew every camp from Brush Creek to Atikokan. A bad jack earned his reputation and found it hard to get a job anywhere, so the only thing he could do was change his name or give up logging. Even then, the word still got around. One sawyer had killed a man over a card game and still worked for many years as a jack. You never knew who was on the other end of the saw.

The foreman figured that I would be a good one to take a chance on, so he hired me on the spot. He showed me where the bunk house was and gave me a spot to store my clothes. The camp was already getting crowded, and the men were double bunked. There was a long plank that ran down the center of each bunk called a snort board. That gave the men a bit of free space from the rollers. Each shack held about 120 men, and there was a big wood stove at each end of the building. Near the stoves were all types of ropes and wires strung around to hang the days wet clothes to dry. The aroma from a two week old pair of socks was something I always remembered.

There was sparse entertainment in the camps, so as a joke for the new jacks, a few of the men sometimes pretended to put on grayback races. They would draw a circle on the floor, and a couple of the men scratched their heads to find the days racers. The resultant letting loose of the lice made for quick conversation and some heavy wagering. Of course, the young jacks let go of some of their hard earned money, and that made it all worthwhile. Occasionally, there was a sore loser, but it was all done in fun.

With the camps not up and running yet, there was far too much spare time, so the boss put the men to work getting firewood or mending harnesses. Trails were cut through the woods to the creeks and rivers. They were preparing for the first snow and cold weather.

Meals were served at the cook shack. The cooks by nature were a sour bunch, and all of them were thought to have been baptized in bad vinegar. It seemed that they hated life, and most of them couldn't cook anything that was fit to eat. They were always run out of camp quickly, and the word was again spread about them. The good cooks, the ones that made good solid food, were highly paid and spoken about as if they were saints. They were indeed a fearsome lot, but no one cared as long as they could cook.

The cook's helper was handed a large tin horn about four feet long, and he walked out the door. He raised it to his lips, and with a great surge of air, produced a sound that was best described as a gawdawful caterwauling racket. No matter what it sounded like, the men recognized it and came on the run.

At the door, hats were removed, and the men immediately became totally silent. There was absolutely no talking allowed, and you were expected to eat quickly and leave.

In the morning, the cook fried up great masses of bacon and sausage, all the while a stump of a pipe dropped ashes onto the food like pepper. They were, with few exceptions, heavy whiskey drinkers that started early in the morning. They produced from the kitchen large pots of oatmeal and pitchers of cream. There were many platters of flapjacks, and right in the very middle of the table was a large bowl with a perfectly round ball of butter. Any jack that thought that he would get much off that butter ball was in for a big surprise. When it was attacked, all it did was roll and be little worse for wear. One of the men, not in too good of a mood one morning, pulled a knife out of his boot and stabbed the butter. At once, the men gave him room. He took what he needed and put the knife back in his boot. The cook decided not to say anything about the incident.

After the first good snows came and the temperature dropped, the logging began in earnest. Trails were made and covered with ice from a water wagon. Nearly all of the trails headed for a stream to take advantage of gravity. The horses, when properly shod with ice shoes, could pull extreme amounts if the trails were iced properly. All of us worked hard or got fired, and there was no time for talking. The two man crews cut many trees in a day, and we earned every bit of pay we got.

At around noon we again heard the cooks horn blowing, and food was brought out to us in small heated sleighs called swingdingles. It was again another quick meal and back to work. Even though the meals were fast, the food was satisfying. The men worked until dark. It was a hard life, and we all worked six days a week.

Evenings again had us eating our meal in silence. There were large quantities of meat and potatoes with lots of hot black coffee. Each night there was a sweet of one kind or another, and most times it was pie. When the supplies ran low, the cook became a bit more creative. Looking through his supplies, he usually had the ingredients to make shoepack pie. A shoepack was a piece of cardboard that you put in your boot to keep your feet warm. After they get a bit soggy, they start to resemble mush, very smelly mush. Shoepack pie was made from many ingredients, none of which resembled cardboard. It was actually quite good and was flavored with lemon, but it did look like a shoepack all the same.

Sunday brought the sky pilot to the camp. We washed our faces and attended a sermon by the traveling parson. He was a little man, so small that he had to stand twice in the same place to cast a shadow.

Fire and brimstone were the stern warnings for the men that wouldn't change their ways. Surprisingly, some of the camp parishioners could actually carry a tune, and the music brought tears to the eyes of some of the family men. A collection plate for his good works usually turned up very few coins. He always remembered which camps paid him well and returned to those often.

Payday was for certain a good reason to celebrate in the logging camps. On Saturday nights, some of the men took the sleigh to town and headed for the saloons. The lovely ladies with their hearts of gold were always ready and waiting for their clients. There were blondes, redheads, and even one that was totally bald from some unknown malady. Between the cheap whiskey and the ladies, the lumberjacks always came back to camp broke, and some came back with things that took quite a while to cure.

Some of us put our money in a sock and worked until spring. Those were always the men with families, like me."

The two men sat and stared at the fire.

"Those were good times, but it was hard not seeing my family for so long at a stretch. We got through it, though."

Chapter 10: Packing Up

Morning found Wil hard at work, packing all of the cured meat into the trailer that he had brought along. There were many small canvas bags that held salted meats, and the dried venison and caribou were packed in wooden crates. Wil didn't really want to leave the company of his new friend, but there was work to do, and the old woman was waiting for him.

As Matt emerged from the tent, he noticed that there was a big change in the camp. The drying racks had been taken down, and the two-man saw was hung back up on the popple tree. There was, however, still the best part of camp, the fire and the coffee. He helped himself and sat down on a block of wood to enjoy the day. The sun was starting to come up over the cattails and there was a quiet chill in the air. The water out on the pond had a dark, almost black look to it. Fall was about to turn into winter. Wil had said last night that his knee was predicting snow again pretty soon.

"I guess it's about time to break camp, Matt. This has been one of the best hunting trips I've had. Little sorry to have to go."

"Same here. I don't think that I'll ever have a hunting trip that will match this one. Going back to the city isn't real appealing either. I am pretty anxious to see my wife, though. She probably misses me by now."

Wil was still loading and was now getting ready to drop the tent. He pulled the center pole, and the whole thing came down with a whoosh. He pulled the stakes and started to fold it back up. This had been home for two weeks, and it looked a bit strange to see his lodge suddenly deflated. Matt came over and helped him fold it up. Once it was put on top of the meat, there wasn't much else to do. The blankets and the rest of his clothes were put into the car. Wil turned to Matt and asked him how much longer he was staying.

"Looks like I'll be right behind you, Wil. Give me a hand with my stuff."

The two attacked the job, and in a half hour, they were loaded up. All that remained was the fire and the coffee. They sat down for one last cup, and both of them were quiet.

"I suppose you'll be back to shaving and doctoring in a day or so."

"I'm not exactly sure about that, Wil. I still have the feeling that I should stay up here."

"Why not come and spend some time with the old woman and me at our cabin. We only live about 120 miles from here, and we've got plenty of groceries from all of our hunting."

They had harvested a large amount of meat. Matt looked at the old man and figured that this was a pretty darned good idea.

"I think I'll take you up on that, Wil, but I do have to call home to let them know what I'm up to. I imagine my wife has given me up for dead by now."

The two drank their coffee, and it seemed that they were both smiling a bit inside. Neither had wanted to leave.

"I'll head out first, and if I make it through the mud holes, you try it. The road looked pretty bad a couple days ago, but it might be frozen by now."

Wil filled the radiator with lake water. He had to drain it every night, but it was cheaper than alcohol. He got in and turned the key and set the throttle. Then, he got out and inserted the crank and gave it a pull. The old car started and died. Another try and it started and kept running.

Matt looked around one last time at the lake. From the time that he arrived nearly two weeks before, he had seen some pretty dramatic changes in himself, and he liked all he saw. He took one last long look at the water and the reeds swaying in the wind. The sky seemed to be completely devoid of ducks now, like they had finished their great migration. He looked out over the lake and saw a single coot paddling circles out near the edge of the reeds. Coots were always one of the very last fliers to use the lake. As he stood there, he noticed that the smells of the swamp were also gone. Things were closing down, getting ready for the big sleep. A moment of sadness swept over him, but it faded fast when he thought of maybe coming back again some day. He got into the car and turned the key, pleased that it fired right up. No cranking for him. His car was a 1940 Ford Coupe and was shiny black. Wil made a run at the road and had no trouble getting through. Matt was right behind him, and off they went toward Wil's cabin and the Bigfork River.

Chapter 11: Ma

When they came to the little town on the Bigfork River, Wil pulled into the general store so Matt could use the telephone. A very pretty young lady behind the counter told him that it would cost him quite a bit to make a phone call to a town so far away. Cost was not the object. His wife needed to know what he was planning and when he was coming home.

The conversation started with Matt smiling, and then there were some silent moments while he just listened, and when he spoke, he spoke softly. The conversation turned to mostly listening, and then he hung up the phone. Matt walked around the store for a few minutes, head hung low. He went to the lady behind the counter and paid for the call.

Matt again walked around the store while Wil spoke to his old fishing partner, the proprietor. He picked out some chewing tobacco and asked for a pound of licorice. He went to the yard goods and asked the lady for enough of her finest dress materials and some thread to make three dresses. The lady threw in some free needles, as she always did. After that, he went to the liquor shelf and took down a bottle of Wild Turkey whiskey, a bottle of dry sherry, and a bottle of good champagne. He gave the lady two twenty dollar gold pieces. She found the correct change, and the two men left the store.

It was a beautiful fall day, and it made the old man's heart glad to be back home on the river. The General Store had been there for a long time and had been enlarged many times as the community grew. It had at one time been painted all white, but now it was a dark gray with small spots of white still showing. They stood on the steps of the general store and looked out over the river. The fall sun was sparkling on the water as it cascaded over the rocks. As they walked toward the cars, Matt didn't have much to say. He stored his purchases in the back and looked at Wil.

"How much farther do we have to go?"

"Oh, not too much farther. We'll be there before you know it."

They drove off down the dusty road and turned into a tall grove of red pines, then up into the woods toward the river. As they came into Wil's place, they saw an old stoop shouldered woman hanging wet clothes on the line. She looked up and saw her husband and walked over to him. He got out of the car and walked toward her. They embraced closely for a while, and Wil kissed his wife softly on her cheek. They walked over to Matt's car, and Wil introduced him to his bride.

"Sure a pleasure to meet you." said Matt.

"And you, too." said Ma. "Come in, and I'll make us a pot of coffee. I think that there might even be some fresh cinnamon rolls about to come out of the oven, too. You get down the coffee grinder, Wil."

They all went into the cabin, and the men sat down at the table. Coffee was a mainstay in most places of northern Minnesota. Even if you had no food in the house, you still had to have coffee.

"Tell me about yourself." said Ma, as she stood by the old Monarch wood stove.

"Not a lot to tell ma'am. I live in Minneapolis, or at least, I used to."

Wil looked at him with a kind of puzzled look.

"I'm a doctor, and I guess pretty busy most of the time, but it sure feels good to be here. Kind of like coming home."

Ma poured some coffee and asked Wil how the hunting was. She seemed to be quite pleased with his report. There were a lot of stories to be told, and Wil was always up to the task.

After some coffee and sweets, the two men walked outside into the yard. They went around the corner and walked down to the river. The water was almost black, and you could toss a rock across it if you had a good arm. Wil said that it was sure good to be back. On the far side of the river, there was a large swamp and beyond that was a big lake. The whole country was beautiful. Wil had watched the water flow by for a lot of years, and it gave him a sense of sameness to see it again. Stability was what he needed this late in his life and no more changes.

Wil and Matt sat down on the hand hewn log bench enjoying the day.

"I'm not quite sure what I'll do now. The wife said the divorce papers will be mailed here, and it should be all over in a month." said Matt.

He hung his head low and got a pained look on his face.

"She said that she found another man that won't up and leave her for weeks at a time. I told her that she could have most everything and to tell the hospital that I won't be coming back."

He had brought some money with him and thought that it might last a while if he were careful.

Wil sat silent for a while, not quite knowing what to say.

"You have a home right here Matt. Ma and I would be glad to see you stay the winter with us. It's been quite a while since we had a third person to play cards with. I doubt that it would take us too long to add another bedroom onto this old cabin."

Matt thought for a short while and then grabbed his friend's arm.

"Thanks, Wil. I think I'll take you up on the offer. I have a lot of thinking to do. I see you already have an extra room, and I'm sure that will work fine for me."

"No. That room is kind of saved the way it is. It used to be our son's room, and nobody ever goes in there anymore."

Wil got up and walked back into the house leaving Matt looking at the river. Ma was extremely excited about the news. Her blue eyes sparkled with elation. It would be like old times, back when the boy was home. In her mind, she was planning the many things that she could cook for Matt. She had to find out what his favorite meals were.

The next day found them all working at putting the meat and hides away for the winter. Ma had gotten out the canning jars and was busy putting up venison in quart Mason jars. Wil hung most of the meat in the smokehouse and root cellar. There were several days of steady work followed by evenings of playing whist. Each evening Wil was the first to call it quits and to head for bed. He seemed to need a lot more sleep than he used to. Matt and Ma sat for a bit and made small talk. She always seemed to have a smile on her face.

Monday morning Wil announced that he knew right where to get the logs for the addition of a new bedroom. It was starting to get pretty cold at night, and they had to get the logs peeled quickly. The work went well, but Matt didn't have any idea of how to work the logs. Wil was a patient teacher, and the student paid close attention. After nearly a week, they had the roof done and the cracks chinked with straw and mud. Matt walked into his new room and thought it was the finest bedroom he had ever seen. He was starting to feel that this was home and that this was where he belonged.

The first night he spent in his new room, it snowed, and the wind blew hard for a while. They had built a straw bed for him, and it fit fine, but it was a lot like sleeping outside in the snow. His talents at chinking left much to be desired. Snow had sifted in through the cracks and there were several small piles of snow on the floor. The day again was spent on improving his new room. He had brought all of his worldly possessions in from the car. There were three pair of pants, three shirts, a pair of shoes, and two jackets. His shaving gear was put on a shelf that he had made, and the three bottles of liquor were set up in the rafters. He hung his Iver Johnson shotgun on a pair of pegs that he fashioned out of cedar. The licorice he gave to Ma to put on the table. He set the new dress material and thread on the bed and the ropes of tobacco on the shelf. Under the bed he put his small black bag with all that he needed to take care of most emergencies. He seriously wondered if he would ever open it again.

With the new day dawning cloudy, it looked like there could be some heavy snow coming soon. The trees barely moved at all, and there were just a few ducks flying by on the river. After a short meal at noon, they noticed a darkening of the sky and looked out the window to see the snow starting to fall in earnest.

"I think winter's here, Ma." Wil said. "I better go and check on the stock."

The two men put on jackets and boots and went to the barn. It was a full twenty degrees warmer inside than outside. There were two Holstein milking cows, six sheep, and stalls for the two draft horses. In the haymow there was enough hay for the stock until spring and new green grass. Everything looked fine, and Wil tossed some hay to the animals. The cattle would be needing another block of salt soon.

"Don't see any problems here, Matt. This is a pretty good barn but the roof needs some patching. One of the center beams needs to be shored up, too. I'd guess that it will make it through another winter."

They headed outside to check on the hogs. They had a small shelter and could make it through most weather. All in all, it seemed that things were in pretty good shape until spring. The snow had started to fall a little more steadily and was covering everything with a coat of fluffy white. They went into the house and had some more coffee. Ma had a rather sober look on her face, and Matt saw that she needed some serious cheering up. He got up from the kitchen table and walked into his bedroom. He took the three new bolts of cloth and thread and brought it out to Ma. The package was wrapped nicely in brown paper, and she got a great smile on her face when she saw it.

"Now what is this young man?"

"Oh, something I found down at the general store."

Oh how she fussed over that small package! There weren't many times in her life when she got to open a gift, and she was going to make the most of it. She finally got a peek at the material and finished opening it quickly. Her eyes lit up like bright new candles. She unfolded it, and the new thread fell out onto the table.

"Even thread! I'm going to have to bring this back to the store. It cost way too much money."

Matt looked into those blue eyes, and he knew that this was a much appreciated gift. He could see the tears well in her eyes.

"Ma, you can make three fine dresses out of that. Now no more talk about taking it back." said Matt.

She grinned and went into their bedroom and came back with some of the pretty cloth wrapped around her like a gown.

"You sure look pretty Ma. It reminds me of when we first met."

Again Matt excused himself from the table and walked back into his new bedroom. He took the ropes of tobacco and hid them behind his back as he walked out into the living room.

"Here, Wil. This is for you."

At first, Wil didn't know what it was, and then, it came to him. It had been quite some time since he had been able to afford such a luxury.

"Thanks, Matt. That's pretty nice of you."

Next morning Matt was up early and out the door to the barn. His first steps were in snow nearly up to his waist, and it was still coming down hard. He fed and watered the stock and thought that he might give milking a try. He had watched Wil do it, and it seemed to be a simple enough task. He got the milking stool and a bucket and got in position to start. He grabbed two handfuls of cow and started to pull on the teats. The cow looked back at him as if to ask, 'who in the world are you?'

After some more pulling, the cow got tired of this foolishness and sent the bucket flying across the barn. Matt got up and retrieved the bucket and tried it one more time with some success. This time he got nearly a quart before the cow kicked the pail over again. He decided to wait a while for Wil and let him do the milking.

He checked on the pigs, and they seemed to be doing alright, too. The chickens were doing fine in their coop, and he picked up nearly a dozen eggs for their breakfast. By the time that he got back to the cabin, his tracks were nearly erased by the windblown snow. This was one of the worst storms that Matt had ever seen.

As he entered the cabin, Ma was standing at the cookstove, and Wil was sitting at the table having his coffee. This time he had cream and sugar in it. He poured it into a saucer and noisily slurped it down. It seemed almost like a dessert to him. Wil looked up and asked how the animals were.

"Seems like they are doing alright, but that sure is a lot of snow coming down. The wind is getting to be pretty bad, too. Oh yeah, how do you milk a cow?"

Both of them looked at Matt and grinned.

"Did you give it a try?" asked Wil.

"Kind of, I guess."

They all had another good laugh at Matt's expense.

"Matt, them pigs might just freeze if we don't let them out. If they can burrow into the straw, I think they'll be alright. The big straw pile is outside the fence though, and I am a bit worried about the wolves getting them."

"The last time I looked, they were nearly buried in snow." Matt said. "If we don't let them out, we'll lose them for sure anyway."

Matt made a path to the straw pile, and the pigs burrowed right in. Not much else that they could do, so they'd have to watch the storm run its course and see what happened.

Matt spent the rest of the afternoon building a fishing rod to catch some of the river's larger residents. He purchased some split bamboo blanks from the general store a couple weeks back and several spools of silk thread to wrap the ferules. He shellacked the whole project and set it up in the rafters to dry slowly. He turned to making some lures. There were many multi-colored feathers from wood duck skins and several sizes of hooks. He pulled some feathers off the skin and wrapped them around the hooks. He tied them with silk thread and again shellacked them. He made several types, and Wil didn't have the heart to tell him that, where they lived, there were no trout so small that they bit on such a tiny hook. The fish here wanted really big meals.

Every once in a while, someone looked outside and came back with a weather report. Wil and Ma had been through this many times, so there were no surprises here.

As they finished their dinner and were cleaning up the table, they heard the bells of a horse drawn sleigh as it came into the yard. Wil opened the door, and there stood a friend and his wife. Mr. and Mrs. Ralph Olson, their next door neighbors from a couple miles away, had stopped in for a visit. This wasn't at all uncommon when a storm hit. People needed to get out for a while to breathe fresh air.

"Come in. Come in." said Wil.

"Thanks, Wil. We stopped by to see if we could borrow a spoonful of sugar. Oh yes, and if you could give it to me in a cup of coffee, it would be surely appreciated."

They all laughed and took off their snow covered coats and hats. Mrs. Olson had a beautiful shawl that was nearly an inch thick with snow. Ma shook it off and hung it near the fire to dry.

"Come and sit a spell." said Ma. "It sure is nice to see you folks."

They all sat at the kitchen table and in short order introduced Matt to their long time neighbors. Winters were tough on all of the people of the Bigfork Valley, but visiting other folks made it much easier to get by. They drank several pots of coffee and played euchre until it was nearly 10:30 p.m. and time to go home. The visit had been quite welcome to them all, and Wil promised to return the favor soon. The sleigh bells rang softly as they left the red pines and disappeared into the night.

The next morning, Matt was up again early to check on the stock, but when he tried to open the door, it wouldn't move. He went to the window, and all he could see was snow. He went to the cook stove and started a good fire to get the coffee going. Soon, Wil came out and Matt explained the situation.

"You know, Matt, this same thing happened quite a few years ago. I tried to get the kitchen door open, and it was frozen shut. After I beat on it for a while, Ma told me just to crawl through the window. I guess she's a might smarter than I am." and they all laughed.

"All you have to do is make a hole through to the sun."

Matt felt that he was up to it, but he had to find a shovel first. Wil told him that there was one next to the door, so he gave it a try. He crawled through the window and into the bluish colored snow. He only had to push upwards a couple inches and a kind of somber looking daylight worked its way into the house. He was only out a short time, and Wil could hear him outside the door shoveling. The snow had drifted onto the side of the house and wasn't that hard to clear. Soon, he was back in the house with his report.

"Wil, there's an awful lot of snow out there! It's piled up onto the north side of the barn, but the small door is clear. It's still coming down, but darn, Wil, it can't keep it up like this forever can it?"

"No. I suppose it can't, but it could keep coming for a couple more days. This is a tough part of the world."

"Do you think that the pigs made it so far? It looks like the straw pile is buried."

"If it doesn't last too much longer, I think they'll be alright."

Both men went to the barn and took care of the chores. Wil did the milking, and Matt fed the stock. Between them, it took no more than two hours until they were back in the house.

The storm kept on for almost all of that day and toward mid afternoon they noticed the sun was starting to come out. The wind was still fierce, but at least, the snow had quit. During the coming night there would be a lot of drifting again, but they could handle it. Wil grabbed a chew of tobacco, and Ma took out her new dress material. They knew how to weather a storm, but Matt had never seen anything like this. Later, Wil grabbed the deck of cards and asked if anyone wanted to play whist.

The storm passed, and in a couple days, all was back to normal. The pigs dug themselves out, and in spite of the severity of the storm and the roving wolf packs, they didn't lose any of their stock.

Chapter 12: Christmas

It was mid December, and the winter was wearing hard on them all. Matt, not used to being cooped up, had been looking for something to keep himself busy. One early afternoon, as he looked around in an old shed, he found some hand tools. There were a brace and bits, a couple different saws and a handful of different shaped chisels. He had been quite a good woodworker at one time, and the thought of building something was very appealing. He went back into the house in the evening and didn't say anything to Wil and Ma about his findings. He was trying to think of something to make them for Christmas.

The next day, he put on a pair of snow shoes and went for a walk. All that Wil had were five foot trail shoes, and he had a hard time getting used to them. He headed out across the river into the bog and found some diamond willow. This was the best wood for making fancy furniture and canes. He hauled as much home as he could carry. Wil saw him head into the shed and didn't think too much of it. His winter evenings were spent working with a coal oil lantern for light. His carving at first took a toll on his thumbs, but in due time, there was less and less demand for blood transfusions. He had some of the wood in a vice being bent for his project, and it had taken him several days to get it shaped the way he wanted it. He drilled and sawed and measured and passed the early winter enjoying himself doing work far less demanding than what he had been trained to do.

Christmas Eve was fast approaching, and Wil and Matt headed to the woods to find their Christmas tree. They searched long and hard for the one that would please Ma most. After an exhaustive scouring of the countryside, they found it and headed back home. They brought it into the barn and built a stand for it. Then they took it inside. Ma inspected it and gave it a nod and her smile of approval. She gave it a special spot in the corner of the cabin and told the men to go back outside and do something useful. She had already taken out all of the old decorations. There were the ones that the twins had made so long ago, and she hung them on the tree with care. She found one that her boy had sent her from Hawaii. She put that on the tree as well. Then, it was the paper chains that she and Wil made the year before. She stood back and admired their tree, thinking of all the days gone by when there were children in the house. Wil and Matt came back into the house, and their vote was unanimous. The tree was absolutely the finest one that they had ever seen. Ma handed Wil that one special ornament, and he placed the star on the very top of the tree.

Christmas Eve arrived with much fanfare, and the house seemed to be a bit more brightly lit and cheerful than usual. Wil had made some nicely colored candles and placed them around the house. Their flickering brilliance made for a very festive atmosphere. There were a variety of special cookies on the table, and Ma brought out the fruitcake that she had been tending for the last four weeks. It was a wonderful time, and they sang Christmas songs until they were all too tired to continue. There was a glass of sherry for each of them and a toast to good health.

They hugged each other and said Merry Christmas. There were few if any dry eyes in the cabin that night, each for a different reason.

Somewhere around midnight, Matt quietly slipped out of the cabin and headed in the dark to the shed. It was extremely cold, and his breath hung in the air like a fog. He reached the shed door and opened it. There on the bench were the fruits of his many hours of labor. He took the first one and quietly made his way to the cabin door. He stepped inside and walked to the hearth. He repeated this again and shut up the doors for the evening. Quietly, he went back into his bedroom and on this special night, he bowed his head. It seemed that he had a very good life once again.

Matt awoke, and the morning light had not yet invaded his room. He heard muffled whispers coming from the candle lit living room, and he slipped into his pants and shirt to go out and see what they thought of their gifts. There he found Wil and Ma sitting in their new rocking chairs near the fire, both of them smiling.

"Matt, I don't think that I have ever gotten such a nice gift." Ma said.

"Me either, Matt. How long have you been working on these? They are beautifully done."

"Well, thank you. I've been working on them for a few weeks now, but it's been hard to hide from you two."

"Here, Matt. This is for you," Ma said.

Matt opened up his package quite slowly and found a new pair of mittens that Ma knitted. She worked on them each time that he was outside. He was most pleased with his gift and put them on right away. Then, Wil handed him a small sack.

"Now what is this?"

He opened the small sack tied with red ribbon and found a handful of spearmint candies.

"Thanks, Wil."

This was indeed the very best Christmas that they could remember.

After some breakfast, Wil walked out to the barn with a special treat for the animals. He had a pocket full of parsnips and carrots for them. His father told him a story a long time ago about how the barn animals became special on Christmas Day. This was a private tradition with Wil.

Later that day, Ma made a fine dinner of roasted crane and mashed potatoes. There was spinach, green beans, harvest rolls, brown gravy, and best of all, sweet potatoes from the general store. They all enjoyed their meal as much as the company, and when each was so full that they could hold no more, Ma brought out a beautiful white cake. It was far too pretty to even cut, so they decided to save it for later that evening.

They figured that they needed some fresh air, so they went out for a walk in the new snow. The trees were all covered with hoarfrost from the open spots on the river, and a few nuthatches accompanied them on their walk, flitting close to them as they walked slowly down the tree lined road. The snow in the woods was already deep, and Wil surmised that the deer might have a tough time of it this winter. They continued to walk down to the main road talking and laughing and turned to go back home.

Ma poked Wil in the ribs and winked at him. She stooped down to grab a handful of snow and packed it into a ball. Wil took the hint and did the same. Since Matt was leading the group, he had no idea what was happening.

"Hey, Matt!" said Ma.

He turned in time to get a face full of icy cold snow that slid right down his neck and into his shirt. He turned his head away, and Wil fired one at the back of his head. In two quick throws, they had reduced the boy to a laughing, snow covered form in dire need of dry clothes. They all laughed, and the fight continued for a bit as they walked back to the cabin. As they got near the door, they stopped to look at the beautiful sight ahead of them. The cabin covered heavily in snow, the smoke curling up from the chimney, and the river behind made for an unforgettable sight in the moonlight.

Later that night as they sat enjoying the fireplace and the cake, each commented on how the others had affected their lives. They agreed that Matt had made their lives much richer in many different ways. When it was time to go to bed, they hugged each other and said many thanks for the gifts and the day.

Chapter 13: Disaster

The winter was wearing on, and spring was getting a bit closer, even though it didn't look that way in the woods. Sometimes at night, Matt could hear the river ice creaking and groaning under the weight of the new season around the corner. The snow that had drifted to the very top of the barn was starting to recede, and the melt was running into the Bigfork River. Each day brought something new. One day it was a spring bird that had returned and the next, it was a flower that was peeking through the wet snow.

Wil asked Matt if he had ever made maple syrup. He handed Matt a spile and asked him if he could carve some of them for gathering sap. He said that he could, and in a couple days, he had carved nearly fifty of them. Wil and Ma had a huge caldron hanging behind the shed. Ma washed it and boiled lots of hot water to clean it. As the sun took the rest of the snow, they started to gather the sap. Wil showed Matt how to drill a hole in the maple tree and drive a spile into it. He hung a bucket or can on each one. The caldron was set on a large iron tripod, and a good fire was built under it. The sap from the trees had to be boiled down to make it sweeter, and that required that someone watch the caldron both day and night. They took turns gathering the sap and watching the fire. As it went down in volume, they replaced it with more sap. By the time that they had tired sufficiently, Ma declared that the caldron's contents were fit to can. She put the sweet maple syrup up in pint jars and set them in the root cellar. Altogether she put up over seventy pints, and that meant that there was still plenty to sell to the general store for cash. Some of the syrup she continued to cook until it crystallized. This she dropped by teaspoons onto the table to cool. This was pure maple sugar candy and a treat for all.

Wil split some oak firewood behind the barn one morning. He took a hard swing at the piece he was splitting and, in a moment of inattention, the axe caught the edge of the wood and went right into his leg. He felt the axe take a bad turn and got it slowed some so it didn't cut him as badly as it could have. It hit him right above the ankle, and he bled profusely. Not being one to complain, he took out his bandana and pressed hard on the large wound to stay the bleeding. It didn't seem to help staunch the blood flow.

He decided that he better get Ma to help him and hobbled to the house, falling inside once he opened the door. He had lost a lot of blood and was starting to get a little weak. Ma helped him into a chair and took a look at the wound. It was deep, and she said that she was going to have to sew it up. About that time, Matt came in and asked where all the blood outside had come from. He didn't have long to wait for his answer. One look at the wound, and he went to his room for the black bag. He came back out, and immediately put on his surgeon face and went to work. After he washed and disinfected the wound with iodine, he took out a syringe and injected the area with Novocain. Next, he took some suture material and stitched up the wound. All the while, Ma was looking over his shoulder and saw the doctor in him emerge. It was a marvelous transformation from a young jackpine savage to a surgeon, and she saw it happen right in front of her eyes. His manner, his voice, and even the way he looked changed in a moment of need.

Wil rested in his bed for a few days and healed. In time the stitches were starting to itch, and Matt knew that the old man would be alright. He ate his share of soup and bread and grew tired of being inside all day. One day Matt came in and asked him if he wanted to get rid of those darned stitches. He was more than happy to oblige. With a few clips and pulls, the stitches were removed. The wound was large, but it healed without difficulty.

That evening as they ate supper, Ma asked Matt if he ever thought about going back to doctoring again. He said that he wasn't sure, but he had been thinking that he might want to. Wil ate in silence that night, not like most times when he had quite a bit to say. He was thinking about the time when Matt might leave the valley, and it bothered him greatly.

The next day Matt walked up to the general store and had a talk with the owner, Mr. Miskovich. He asked if he had any space that he might want to rent to him. The man said that he didn't, but he did know about a piece of land that was next to the store, a good place for an office. Matt thought about it for a while and asked for the owner's name. It was a man by the name of Oscar Robinson, and he lived a short distance from town. Since it was such a nice day, Matt walked down the road to the Robinson's home and knocked on the door.

A beautiful woman answered the door, and he remembered seeing her before at the general store. He was caught speechless for a moment. This had to be the prettiest woman that he had ever seen. Matt asked if this was the Robinson's home, and she said that it was. He asked if the owner of the land next to the general store was around. She said that he was out back in the shed making a lot of racket with a hammer, and she laughed. Matt walked around the house and found the noisemaker in the back, building a rocking horse for his grandson. He surmised that the beautiful woman must be married.

Matt introduced himself to the man and said that he was interested in purchasing the property next to the general store. The man said that the price was high because he knew that someday this town would grow. He gave a price of twelve hundred dollars, and the doctor thought that it was close to what he wanted to pay. They made a deal, and after the customary bit of haggling, they agreed on a price of eleven hundred dollars. Matt asked what he was building, and he said that his daughter and son-in-law were coming from Nebraska. All of a sudden it came to Matt that the beautiful woman might still be unmarried.

They agreed on a date of possession, and Matt left with the bill of sale in his hand. Thoughts were running through his mind like a fast river. He was trying to think of an excuse to go back and talk to her for a while, but he couldn't come up with a good reason to knock on the door. He had heard her father call her Jane.

Chapter 14: The Cabin

Summer was passing slowly, and the garden was starting to show some promise. Wil had tended it carefully, and each year's harvest gave him a sense of accomplishment. It was hard work, but he enjoyed it. One day as he hoed the potatoes, an old friend named Joe Barrett walked into the yard looking for him.

"Wil, I need your help. We're building a new cabin for my son Frank and his wife, and we're about tuckered out. We need to find a few good men to finish it up, and I thought that you might lend a hand."

Wil's eyes brightened up.

"I heard that there was one being built up river a ways. I wasn't sure whose land it was on though."

"Yup. That's the place. We have just a few days work left, and they could move in."

Wil agreed to give a hand, and Matt said he'd go along for the experience. They put a couple axes and a good saw into the canoe and pushed off. Wil and Matt paddled well together and were making good time. When they arrived at the new cabin site, they pulled the canoe in and headed uphill to see how it was going.

"Hi, Joe," Wil said. "I brought along Matt to give a hand. Besides, Ma said that if he didn't find something to do to keep busy, she was going to teach him how to knit."

That drew a laugh from them all.

Wil walked behind the cabin and looked it over. He doubted that he had ever seen such a mess in all his life. There was no amount of chinking that could seal up cracks that big. Just walking near the cabin was a hazardous undertaking. It was in need of being torn down and started over. He didn't know how to say it to Joe. Wil started to open his mouth to talk, and Joe butted right in.

"You know, Wil, I don't think I've ever seen such a mess in my life. All we can do is start over."

That took the pressure off Wil, and he nodded in agreement. The dismemberment project didn't take very long, and it seemed that it was a blessing because a strong wind would have done the job anyway. The big logs came down with a hard thud and rolled out of the way. In half an hour, they were right back to where they started except that the floor was still acceptable to use. The men started over, notching the logs one at a time to fit the one beneath. By the time noon arrived, the men were tired and hungry. The walls were nearly up four feet and not much air showed between them. Joe seemed to be pretty pleased with the whole project.

By evening they had only raised the walls another couple feet. The higher they went, the harder it was to roll the big logs in place. The horses worked hard with each log, and progress was starting to show even though it was slow in coming.

"Time to head home for the day," said Joe. "I'm plum tuckered out. The boy will be here tomorrow, and he'll stay with it until we're done and he's moved in."

"Let's go, Matt. We'll hit it hard again tomorrow."

Joe thanked the men and watched them disappear down river. He turned and looked at the cabin. It was sure a nice place for a home. A little far from the school for kids, but it would be some time before they needed to worry about that.

The next day, Wil and Matt came back to finish the walls. Frank was quite surprised to see how far they had come on the project. With a fresh supply of energy, they tackled the logs with renewed strength. As day wore on, they were nearing the last course of logs. When the last one clunked in place, they all cheered. They had done the hard part, and now it was time to figure out some kind of a roof. They had figured to make a frame of logs and cover that with boards from the mill. It sounded like a pretty good plan, except that there was no road close to the cabin with the nearest one being a quarter mile away.

Again the men had their work cut out for them. They took the team of horses and started to clear a straight line to the road. At the end of another day, they had cleared enough brush to nearly qualify as a road. It was a grueling task, and the men were completely exhausted at the end of another day. This was starting to seem a lot like work. As close as he could figure, it was almost another whole week's labor before they could move in.

That evening Ma asked Wil how the job was going, and both men were too tired to talk about it. To Ma, Wil looked a little worse for wear, but he could handle a day's work without complaining.

After a few more days labor, the roof was in place, and they were busy digging a pit for the outhouse. The deer flies were out in force, and what they didn't bite, the mosquitoes did. All the men were covered with bites or stings of one sort or another.

The next job was to dig some sort of a well, and this was a job that nobody cared for. Wil cut a green willow fork and went to work witching for water. Joe and Frank started to laugh at Wil, saying that he had never seen such a thing. As he walked, the fork in Wil's hand started to bend to the ground. Wil tried hard to keep the fork straight, but the pull of the water twisted the bark right off in Wil's hand. The grin left Joe's face. Near as Wil could figure, the best place was about twenty feet from the cabin door. It was a great place for a well.

There was always the danger of the well caving in on someone. They started to dig, and each man took a turn in the hole. They had gotten only about six feet deep and the walls of the well caved in on Frank nearly up to his waist. There were a few minutes where they stood thinking. Wil figured that the investment in some pipe might save a life. Open wells had claimed many children anyway. They took the team and went to the general store and purchased forty feet of two inch pipe and a sand point to drive into the ground. Wil picked up a few drive couplings and borrowed the heavy driving weight from the store. They picked out a cistern pump, and they were nearly in business.

After they got back to the cabin, they rigged a high tripod and a large pulley. They lifted the weight and let it drop onto the drive coupling. It was pretty slow going, but when they reached twenty-four feet, the pipe filled with water. Wil knew that a well would take as much water as it would give, so they started to pour buckets of water into the pipe. The faster they poured the faster the water disappeared. This had the makings of being a darned good well.

They cut off the casing and attached the cistern pump, complete with rods and foot valves. Joe started to pump the handle. The water came out in great gushes and filled the bucket in short order. After pumping steadily for several minutes, they each took a turn trying out the new water to see if it was fit to drink. It was pure clean water, and Frank smiled in approval.

They sat down on a log, trying to figure what was next. There was an awful pile of stumps left in the yard, but Joe and Frank could dig them out in time.

"Men," said Joe, "I got to thank you for all your hard work. My son has a fine new home with good water.

They all agreed with Joe and went on home to tend to their own chores. It had been more than a week's hard work, but it was what neighbors did for one another.

Summer was turning close to harvest time, and the raspberries were producing enough to keep Ma busy canning all day. The finished product was lined up on the table, and they thought of how good it would taste in the middle of winter. Wil had a liking for berries and cream, especially if Ma made some good shortcake to go with it.

Wil was busy one day in the barn when Joe and Frank Barrett drove into the yard with a team of horses. Joe asked if Wil had ever used dynamite. Wil said that he had, but it was dangerous work and best left to a powder man.

"What in the world are you going to blow up?"

"Well, we got a few big stumps left out at the cabin, and they just won't move. We worked on them for a couple days each."

"I do know how to rig the stuff, but that's a little close to the house for using dynamite. I think you'd be better off to use the horses."

"Nope. We done about as much shoveling as we're going to. I need you to show me how to set the blasting caps."

With that, Joe walked to the wagon and got out some sticks of dynamite and handed them to Wil. Wil looked a bit shaken, trying to figure how much trouble Joe could get into with this stuff. Joe gave him a blasting cap and asked Wil to show how it was done. Wil figured that Joe was serious now and decided to cooperate with him.

"Well, you wrap tape around a couple sticks and push the blasting cap inside the dynamite. You cut a long fuse and set it under the stump, light the fuse and run. It'll probably shake the windows in the cabin and loosen the dirt around the stump. You'll be able to pull it out with the team of horses."

Joe seemed to be satisfied with the instructions and thanked him. They got back onto the wagon and headed out to the cabin to finish off the stumps, leaving Wil behind shaking his head.

When Joe got to the cabin, he sized up the first victim and put two sticks under the first stump. He lit the fuse and ran behind the wood pile. When it went off, Joe was a little surprised that it didn't make more noise. It made a low kind of "whump" sound. He went to check on the stump and found dirt had sprayed nearly everywhere, but the stump was still right where he left it. However, it did look a bit worse for wear and came out with only an hours digging. He figured that it was a sure success.

The next stump was quite a bit larger so Joe figured that about six sticks were needed for such a chore. He wrapped them carefully with tape and dug a small hole under the stump for the explosive.

Back down the river at Wil's place, he had heard the first charge go off and had to go and see what had happened. As he neared the cabin, he saw Joe hunkered down behind the wood pile and figured that it was about to blow again. Wil was still a couple hundred yards from the cabin, but he saw it all. Joe had his fingers in his ears nearly up to his elbows. When the charge went off, Wil didn't even have time to blink. There was a bright flash followed immediately by a loud bang, and then he saw it. A large stump was in the air, rising to unheard of heights. It reached its peak and started to come back down. As it disappeared back into the cloud of smoke and dirt, he heard another sound that seemed to be more of a crashing noise. This was getting to be more than Wil could handle, and he walked up to Joe.

"I think you used a bit too much on that one, Joe."

Joe agreed and said that he might have to be a bit more careful from now on, but the stump was after all gone.

They walked into the cabin to have a cup of coffee, and there in the middle of the living room was the wayward stump, still smoking. He had gotten it out of the ground alright, but nearly destroyed the house in the process. Wil saw the look on Frank and Joe's faces and busted out in fits of laughter that could have been heard for miles. All thoughts of coffee faded as Wil bent double shaking in convulsions. Each time that it would start to subside some, he'd look at Joe and start in all over again. Joe, however, was having some difficulty finding much humor in his situation.

Chapter 15: New Beginning

Matt eventually worked up enough courage to go and knock on Jane's door one evening. They sat on the porch and just made small talk for a while with Jane's parents sitting with them. Jane wanted to know all about his time in medical school, and Matt wanted to know about her life here on the river.

There was a dance coming up, and as soon as Matt heard about it, he asked Jane if she would like to go. She blushed and said that she would.

Matt prepared for the big event with a haircut and a bath. Nothing was spared for this first date, and he even bought some flowers for Jane. The evening came, and Matt knocked on the door at the appropriate time.

"Come in, Matt." said Mr. Robinson. "Seems like we see you a bit more often nowadays."

"Thanks, Mr. Robinson. Is Jane ready to go to the dance?"

"Oh, she'll be right down. Now don't be in such a rush."

The two sat and made small talk for quite a while with Matt glancing at his watch several times. It seemed to Matt that he was seriously early, or Jane was seriously late. Then he heard voices, and the prettiest woman in the world came into the room with her mother. Matt jumped up when he saw her and nearly knocked over the coffee table.

"Hello, Jane. You sure are pretty. Hello, Mrs. Robinson. I got these flowers for you, Jane"

"Hello, Matt. Thank you. These are beautiful. Are you about ready to go?" said Jane.

They started for the door, and Mr. Robinson stood in Matt's way.

"What time are you going to have Jane home?"

"I'll have her home before midnight if that's alright with you."

"That'll be fine, but make sure you do."

They walked outside, and Jane gave out a big laugh as the door closed.

"Dad's just trying to make you nervous." Jane said.

"It worked just fine." said Matt in a voice that was still a bit shaky.

The season found Matt and Jane together as much as their busy schedules would allow. Sundays were spent either with Jane's family or Matt's. The community now thought of them as a couple.

Matt and Wil worked hard building the new office. There was an operating room with bright lights and an examination room. Nearly all of the money that Matt had with him went into the new office, and he was very proud of his accomplishment. By the end of August, he had his shingle on the door and his first patient, a woman who was about to give birth. Her husband arrived at the office on horseback and told Matt the situation. The doctor hurried to get his things together and stopped at the Robinson's to ask Jane if she would come along to help. The outcome was in doubt because she was an older woman and had never had any children. Her husband was there, too. He held his wife's hand throughout the entire ordeal. After many hours of difficult labor, she gave birth to a baby boy. The mother was in pretty bad condition and needed to be nursed back to health. Matt asked Jane if she would stay there with the new mother for a couple days. She said that she would, and Matt was quite pleased. He thought for a moment that he might have found his new nurse.

Matt left to go back to the office. It was near midnight, and the sky was full of stars. As he drove along, he reflected on the day and the help that he had been given by Jane Robinson. She seemed to have a feel for helping others. She had never been a midwife, but there are certain things that a woman knows. In addition to that, she was still about the prettiest woman he had ever seen.

He stopped into his office to see if there were any messages hung on his door. Seeing none, he continued on down the road toward home. It seemed to be so peaceful here. The men and women were all friendly and hard working. Neighbor helped neighbor, and that made life go better for all. The whole community had welcomed Matt, and he, for certain, felt that this was now his home.

When he got to the cabin, he opened the door and there was Wil sitting in his rocking chair looking into the flames.

"Sit down for a spell, Matt. I haven't seen you in a while."

Matt sat down by the fire, and the two friends talked for a time. Matt might be the community's doctor now, but his family was still the most important thing in his life. Wil was his friend and mentor, teaching him all he needed to know to make a life here on the Bigfork River. They talked a while about the farm, breeding stock, fishing, and even about the hunting trip coming in October. Wil assumed that Matt would be hunting this fall, and that was fine with him. On the mantel above the hearth stood a picture of two small boys, obviously twins, and a picture of his son that he had lost in the war. Matt noticed something behind the boys picture. It was a Prince Albert tobacco can. He knew that Wil didn't smoke and wondered what was in it. He wanted to ask the old man, but thought better of the idea.

Late August brought ricing season, and a chance to not only put away food for winter, but to sell some wild rice to the folks in the big cities. They all had a taste for it and paid dearly for its wonderful flavor, especially when served with wild game. The ricing wasn't actually that hard, but it took a lot of time. Matt was more than willing to give it a try, but he had to start off by poling, the hardest part of the process.

Wil and Matt started out the first morning paddling around looking at the different rice beds to see which was ripe and ready to harvest. The rice heads were full, but still in the milk stage where it was soft and held a lot of water. It easily rotted before it could be processed. The next two beds showed that they were close to being ready. The best rice beds were in protected areas where the water level stayed much the same throughout the year. The water was only a foot or two deep, but still deep enough to get real wet if the poler wasn't careful. Wil figured it would be two days until they could start.

That evening Wil and Matt checked out the equipment and figured that they needed a new pole. It had to be about sixteen feet long and a good solid three pointed fork at one end so it wouldn't stick in the river mud. Matt knew what he wanted and went to the woods to get the right one. He peeled it and sanded it down so it was easy on his hands. Wil went into the barn and got out twenty feed and flour sacks to put the rice in and picked up his sticks. The sticks were about thirty inches long and pointed at one end. He had used the same ones for many years, and he liked the feel of them. It looked like the canoe was still in pretty good shape and wouldn't need any work at all. He had painted it inside and out last year.

The day they started ricing, the sun had risen bright and warm. Wil got into the canoe, and Matt stepped in as if he was getting aboard a steamship. The result was an overturned canoe and two very wet men. Wil came up spluttering, and Matt stood in the water wondering what had happened. Wil looked at him and shook his head.

"Dammit, boy," he spluttered. "You have to be more careful."

Matt looked at him, and they both started to laugh again. Wil saw his favorite picking sticks floating down the river, and Matt headed for them swimming strongly. Wil pulled the canoe up onto the bank and threw out the wet sacks. They both headed to the house for dry clothes. Ma looked at them and said that it had been quite a short trip.

In an hour, they had everything back the way it was before the first attempt, and Wil taught Matt the right way to get into a canoe. He felt a bit sheepish and took the lessons to heart. They paddled for a while until they got into the first rice bed. Wil again instructed Matt on how he had to keep the canoe in the best rice. He was standing and could see all the best places. Soon they were moving in good rice, and the picking began. At first it was a bit slow, but in a short while, there was a good layer of rice on the bottom of the canoe. Wil reached with his left stick and pulled a nice bunch of rice over the side of the canoe, and with the other stick, he knocked the ripe kernels off and into the canoe. Whitt chuk chuk. Whitt chuk chuk. There was a real rhythm to it, and it sounded to Matt almost like a heartbeat. Matt placed the pole into the water and gently guided the canoe along back and forth in the rice. It was hard work, but they were doing well.

Within very few minutes, Matt felt something crawling on his leg and bent down to have a look. His pants, inside and out, were covered with little half inch long green rice worms. Wil hadn't told him this part, but it went along with ricing. There were huge flocks of red-winged blackbirds moving in and out of the rice eating whatever they could find, mostly the small rice worms. Another thing to be careful about were the rice beards. Neither man wore glasses so in a short time, Matt noticed that Wil was rubbing his eyes. He had picked up a rice beard, and they hurt like sin itself. Matt dipped his hands in water to clean them and removed the beard from Wil's eye. If let go, rice beards could cause blindness.

They went past a small area that had a black fungus on the rice. Some of it had an irregular heavy growth and made the stalks bend over. Wil wouldn't pick near it. As they passed by, Matt's curiosity got the best of him and he asked what it was.

"Ergot. The Indians used to smoke it, and they would see visions, and it was also used to make a woman end a pregnancy."

Matt thought on this for a while and his scientific training made him try to identify what could have been in it.

Within an hour, they had a canoe nearly half filled with rice, so they stopped to bag it up. It felt good to Wil to stretch his legs. They had four good bags of rice already, and it appeared to be good quality.

As the day wore on, the canoe held about all they could carry, so they headed back home for the day. The men unloaded the canoe and spread the rice out to dry in the sun. In a couple days, the rice would be parched in the big cauldron.

Preparations were made to process the rice. A fire was built under the cauldron, and a bucket of rice was thrown in to parch. Wil grabbed a canoe paddle and stirred it around making sure that all the rice got parched equally. The rice was poured out on deer hides and cooled. Next came the fun part. Wil asked Matt if he'd like to dance.

"I never danced with a man before, but if you can hum a tune, I'd give it a try." Matt said laughing.

"No. Not that kind of dancing."

There was a long pole extending over a slight depression in the ground. A large hide was used to keep the rice clean. Wil poured a bucket of parched rice on the hide and handed Matt a clean pair of moccasins.

"This is a jig pole, and this is called jigging the rice. Hold onto the pole for balance and dance on the rice to remove the hulls. Do you think you can do it?"

"Sure."

The jigging wasn't that hard, but there was an awful lot of rice to do. After it was all done, there was a combination of hulls and good rice all mixed together. Wil had a shallow basket about a foot and a half across. He poured some rice in the basket and threw it high in the air catching the rice as it came back down. The chaff blew away with the evening breeze. All that was left after a couple hours was the finished rice and a smiling family.

The ricing continued as the crop ripened, and Matt was getting pretty good at it. Eventually, Wil allowed Matt to try picking. He was quite clumsy at first, and the rice flew everywhere except in the canoe. It took him quite a while to get the hang of it. As they poled along in silence, they heard something, and Wil stopped. The sound grew somewhat louder, and then he saw where it was coming from.

There were two Indian women coming toward them in their canoe. They were singing as they picked rice. The tempo of the song was matched by the knocking sticks. The song was eternal, and all the Anishinaabe knew it from childhood. Wild rice was a large part of their diet, and they put away many hundreds of pounds of it for the winter. They waved at Wil, and he recognized them as old friends from the town of Redby not far away on Red Lake.

Wil and Matt finished the ricing. They took the extra rice to the general store and sold it to a rice buyer from the big city. The price wasn't as good as last year, but the crop was better so they did well anyway. Ma had several dollars to spend on things for herself and the house, and Wil bought a new pair of boots. Matt took his share and bought a new double barreled shotgun. That took all his money but four dollars. With that, he bought a gift of candy for Jane, his friend and sometimes nurse.

Chapter 16: A Serious Proposal

One evening as they played whist, Matt mentioned that he had a friend who bought cranberry bark that they used in making a certain medicine. This sparked an interest in Wil, and he mentioned that he knew where to get tons of the stuff. The next day Matt wrote to his old friend and asked about buying the bark from Wil. In due time, Matt got back a letter with a contract for Wil to sign. It stated that he was to supply them with at least two hundred pounds of bark annually, but no more than five hundred pounds. The price was twenty-seven cents a pound plus the shipping charges. This was a golden opportunity for Wil, and he eagerly signed the contract.

The next day found Wil on the other side of the river inspecting the old cranberry bog. The sky was a bright burning blue and big puffy clouds rolled through headed east toward Lake Superior. As he looked around at the large amount of cranberry plants, he noticed that this year the blueberries, too, were good. These berries came and went, and it usually took a forest fire to make them produce very much. This was also going to be a good year for the big blackberries where last year's running wildfire had scorched the forest. He had picked berries there for years, and the supply was endless. Many times while picking berries, he had to share a favorite spot with the bears. They weren't afraid of him, and the feeling was mutual. One time, he had set his berry bucket down by his foot and looked down in time to see the whole thing get hauled away by a small cub. He didn't think it a good idea to go after it since the sow was only a couple feet away.

Wil started his cranberry bark harvest by tying the four foot canes in bundles. When he had a load, he paddled back across the river and stacked them in the sun to dry. By the time evening came, he had a pile that was five feet high and extended for nearly forty feet. He continued his efforts for another week, and there was no way to determine how many pounds of bark he had.

Matt came in late from the office one evening, and the two went to look at the stack. Matt estimated that he had about a hundred pounds of bark when it was all dried. The truth of the matter was that it ended up to be over six hundred pounds. The pile was gradually disappearing, but it took many days to finish the work. Ma and Wil had sore hands when it was over, but the resultant fortune was sorely needed. It would get them through the winter and more. The good part was that they could do it each year and that was surely welcome.

Ma, Wil, and Matt sat at the kitchen table one morning eating breakfast. The talk on this day was a bit more animated than usual. Matt joked a lot of late, which Ma enjoyed. Matt turned a bit more serious for a moment and asked if he could bring a friend to dinner some night soon. Wil looked up and with a grin on his face said that he knew who it would be too. Ma beamed as well because she knew, too. Matt hadn't said much about Jane Robinson, but each time Ma went to the store for the mail, she heard that something had been going on. Matt had been buying sweets and pretty things for Jane, and it seemed that the whole world knew it. There were few secrets in a small community. Ma thought about it for a while and said that tonight would be good, and Wil agreed. Matt asked what time to bring her, and it was agreed that four o'clock was fine, and that gave them time to talk before dinner.

The day passed in a frenzied pitch for Ma. She had been cleaning all day and cooking some of the many things that Matt liked. They would have baked ham with a honey mustard glaze. She knew that everyone liked that. Then she baked a raisin spice cake with coffee frosting. The smell of the cake lit up the house nicely. Wil walked in and tried to cut a piece for himself and darned near lost an arm for his efforts. Ma grinned at him, and he settled for a sandwich made with some hot ham.

The afternoon wore on, and then they both heard Matt's car coming down the driveway. Jane and Matt held hands as they walked toward the house and that pleased Ma. Jane walked in and gave Ma a big hug.

"It's so good to see you, Jane!" Ma exclaimed. "You're as pretty as ever."

Jane most certainly was a pretty girl who had blossomed late in her teenage years. Before that, she played the role of the tomboy to hide her feelings that she was plain. Her teeth had come in somewhat crooked, and the boys teased her, at least until she started to get real pretty. As they got through school, they wanted to date her, and she had no part of the boys that used to make her feel so bad. So she stayed at home with her Mother, learning all of the things that would make her a great wife for some lucky man. She had turned into a rare beauty, and Matt was totally infatuated with her.

Jane blushed a bit and asked if she could help with dinner. The offer was accepted, and the two women set the table and put on the food. Dinner was delicious, and there was so much of it. Matt ate slowly to impress Jane with his manners. His hair was neatly trimmed, and he was closely shaven. Anyone could tell that it was done for his lady friend. Wil asked how her folks were, and Jane replied that they were both fine. Small talk continued throughout the meal, and finally as they sat having their last bit of coffee, Matt asked if he could make an announcement. He had their attention and proceeded.

"Ma and Wil," he said hesitating for effect, "I'm going to ask Mr. Robinson for Jane's hand in marriage, and we wanted you to be the first to know."

Jane blushed, and Ma put her arms around her.

"I knew it! I knew it! You been a little quieter than usual, Matt, and I knew something was happening. I'm so happy."

It was Wil's turn.

"Jane, I've known you since you were a baby, and I watched as you grew into a young lady. Now you're a beautiful woman and look at you! You are going to be part of our family. Well, it's just plain wonderful."

Jane had her turn.

"I want you to know that I think the world of Matt, and I'll do my best to be a good wife to him. We don't know where we're going to live yet, but we both want to stay here in the woods, close by the river."

Wil didn't even take time to talk to Ma, he blurted it out.

"You can have that forty down the river a bit. I haven't even looked at it now for the last ten years. There's a good high spot for a house, and I don't think the well will be that deep either. There's enough good pine right on the place to build a cabin."

He was ready to start clearing land before the cake was served.

"Whoa, Wil." said Matt. "We haven't even set a date yet. We might not get married for a couple years yet." He looked over at Jane and saw a shadow cross her face, and it was right back to sunshine again.

"I still have to get my practice going a little better, and I'm pretty short of money right now."

The evening's dinner left them all a bit tired, and Matt said that he was going to take Jane home. It was getting on toward 8:00 p.m., and Wil was nodding off in his rocking chair. Jane went over to Wil and gave him a big hug.

"Thank you both for such a nice welcome."

They went out and got into the car. The drive home was pleasant, and they both made small talk.

Matt walked her to the door and kissed her gently.

"Thanks for coming to dinner, Jane. They sure like the idea of us getting married, and so do I."

"Me too. I know we'll have a good life. Goodnight, Matt."

"Goodnight."

Later, when Matt returned to the cabin, Wil was waiting for him in his usual place, near the fire. Matt sat down with him, and the two stared into the flames, like they had done so many times before.

"You know, Matt, you shouldn't keep a lady waiting too long for marriage. Once the words have been said, there's no time for hesitating. If I was you, I'd set a date right close, like next week. You don't want one of those young bucks making a pass at her."

Matt knew about a young man that built up a big logging business in International Falls, and he always stopped in to see her when she was working at the store. A couple times he had forgotten to buy anything at all, and that made her think of him as a suitor. Sometimes she blushed at his comments on how pretty she was.

That got Matt to thinking, and he walked off quietly to his room, pausing a moment to say "goodnight." He sat down on his bed and put his head in his hands.

Wil was about to go to bed when he saw Matt walk from his room and out the door without a word. He didn't think too much of it. Wil figured that he was headed for the outhouse to read the catalogue. He heard the car start and leave the driveway.

Matt arrived at Jane's house in a few minutes and saw that there were still lights on in the house. He walked to the door and knocked. Mr. Robinson opened the door and asked Matt to come in.

"I need to talk to you Mr. Robinson, privately."

"Will the porch be alright?"

"Sure." said Matt, and they walked back outside and closed the door. They no more than sat down, when Jane opened the door.

"I thought I heard your voice, Matt. What's the matter?"

"I need to talk to your dad, privately."

She gave one of her special grins and walked back in and shut the door.

"I want to marry your daughter," Matt said with a shaky voice. "I'll do my best to make her a good husband."

"Fine with me, but don't you think that you should talk to Jane about it first?"

With that they both laughed and got into some serious conversation about their plans. Mr. Robinson was a good man and liked the idea of having Matt as a son-in-law. He wanted a grandson, and he didn't want to wait all of his life for one.

"Ma, come out here for a bit. I got something to tell you."

The lady of the house came out with a big grin on her face.

"I know already. You can't keep this sort of thing secret from a mother."

Jane appeared in the doorway and put her hand on Matt's shoulder.

"We might not be getting married for quite a while though. We need to get Matt's practice going before we do that." Jane said.

"Jane, do you think that next week would be too soon?"

Her composure was totally shaken, but she didn't let it show. "Not at all, Matt."

She threw her arms around Matt and hugged him fiercely. Her voice sounded calm, but inside her heart was racing. Mrs. Robinson cried tears of joy, and Matt grinned broadly.

His ride home was interrupted by a short stop at the rapids to give him a bit of time alone to think. He had met Wil just a year before, and it seemed that they had adopted him. They gave him a place in their house and their hearts that was usually reserved for family. Now, Matt was going to bring a new wife into their circle. It seemed that things were moving fast, but that was the way he did things.

Again he started the car and went on home. He quietly walked into the house and to his room. He sat on the bed again, thinking about the past hours goings on.

Morning found Wil busy making coffee as he usually did. Matt greeted his old friend and poured some coffee for them both.

"We decided that next week was about right."

Wil grinned and drank his coffee. Ma walked out of the bedroom and sat down at the table with the men folk. She wasn't used to such big smiles so early in the morning.

"You both look like you swallowed the canary. Now what's this all about?"

Chapter 17: Preparations

The following days were filled with a flurry of activity. Wil had written a letter to the paper inviting everyone to their big wedding to be held above the rapids on the Bigfork River. It was all set for the next Sunday afternoon. The preacher had been talked to, and they had chosen a best man and a bridesmaid. There would be a potluck dinner afterwards and dancing with real musicians. The cost of the extravaganza was starting to be a bit more than he could handle. Matt hadn't even bought the ring yet, and the big day was drawing near.

As they sat down to dinner that night, Matt started to tell Wil and Ma about his cash problems. The cost of the music had taken most of his cash, but it was something that a community doctor had to do. Ma said that the food wouldn't cost much since it was potluck, and he already had a nice suit to wear. They tallied it all together and figured that he could do it, all except for the ring.

Wil looked over at Ma and gave her a wink. They had hoped to be able to help the boy out in some way, and now they had it figured out. Wil got up from the table and went to the mantel. There behind the picture of a young seaman was the dusty Prince Albert can. Wil took it down with care and looked at it for a bit. Then he opened it up. It hadn't been opened for a long time, and the contents were there just as he had left them. There were numerous ten dollar bills and three twenty dollar bills. All tolled, it was $180.00 even.

"Here, Matt. This is a gift from us. There's a long story behind it, but we want you to have it. There's enough to buy a nice ring for Jane."

Matt looked at the money and over to Ma. The tears were streaming down her face, and she was smiling. Wil reached over to Ma and put his arm around her. All that remained of the family were gathered together in the kitchen, all three of them.

Matt made a trip to International Falls that day and bought a ring for Jane. It was shiny gold with one small diamond in the middle. The man at the store guaranteed that it would please any bride. Matt was quite sure that it would.

Time wound down to a final few days. There were patients to see, and last minute things that needed attending. He spent a lot of time polishing his shoes so that he looked just right. His suit needed pressing, and his hat had to be cleaned.

He saw Jane for a moment on Thursday at his office. There were a couple of lumberjacks that came in with a great number of wounds. Somehow they had gotten into a terrible fight over who could drink the most whiskey. They had decided to have a little contest, and the loser accused the winner of cheating because he spilled some on his chest. They laughed and seemed to be pretty good friends now, but a short while before, it looked a lot like there would be a funeral for sure. One had a very large laceration on his ear, and his nose was bitten hard too, chewed on by the other patient. Jane cleaned one lumberjack's wounds and passed him on to Matt so that he could stitch them up. In an hour, the team had them all put back together, except for the missing piece of one ear, and Matt presented them with a bill for his services. They were each charged five dollars and thought that it was way too much. After much caterwauling, Matt agreed that the price was probably a bit too high and instructed the taller of the two to sit back up on the table. He did as he was told, and Matt went into the corner to wash his hands again. He returned with a small scissors and told the man to let him know when he had removed enough stitches to get to a more reasonable price. The jack was incredulous and took a five dollar bill from his pocket and paid him. After a quick whisper to his friend, he, too, coughed up a five for the doctors services. Out the door they went and across the street to Dirty Annie's for another drink. Matt and Jane shook their heads and proceeded to clean up the mess left by the two woodsmen.

Friday as Matt sat at the table eating breakfast, he asked Ma where Wil was. She said that she heard him a while back as he left the house. He continued with his breakfast and walked outside to see what the old man was up to. He looked in the barn and found that

Wil had already been there and had done all of the chores. Same thing in the chicken coop, and the hogs were fed as well. Still no idea what had happened to Wil. Matt went back inside and got cleaned up and shaved for the day. When he walked back out to the kitchen, there was Wil drinking a big cup of hot coffee. He had been walking to that forty acre spot that he told Matt he could have. There was a large number of logs that were pretty good for a roomy cabin, and the spot was even better than he remembered.

"It looks like there is a large amount of red pines there that will work well for the cabin. They're all straight as an arrow, too. Come on with me, Matt."

Matt and the old man walked down the road and entered the big grove of red pine. Matt was astounded at the size and straightness of the big timber. It looked like a tremendous job to him, but to Wil, it was another part of life on the river. Newlyweds need a place of their own. He had already been to the general store and talked to a bunch of friends and neighbors about a house raising. This was quite a bit the same as a barn raising, and all of the work was laid out so that the men could do it in a day or two. Matt and Wil staked out the size of the house using twine and stepped into the house to see what it felt like. The kitchen would be here, and the bedrooms over there, as Jane and he had planned.

Matt heard the sound of a truck coming down the road. The two jacks he had sewn up the day before got out of the cab. There were ten more tough looking men in the back of the truck. Most of them he recognized from the town. All of them came up to Matt and congratulated him and slapped him soundly on the back. A car stopped, and four more men got out. He looked down the road, and there were eight more men walking toward them. Matt had never heard of such a thing. These men were here to build a cabin for him and Jane, and they would do it in one day.

The work started by picking out which trees would be felled first. Wil went back and got the team of horses. As each tree came down, Wil hooked onto it, and the team pulled it to where it could be peeled. With pike poles they turned the timber so that all sides were done.

Some of the men finished the floor just as the first log was to be set. Axes, saws, and pickeroons flew in all directions, and the men did little resting.

Ma and Jane walked down to see what was happening, and each decided that they could be best used by cooking food for all the men. Jane was very excited to see so many men working on the cabin. Their home was getting closer to becoming a reality.

After the first log was set, the second was ready to be notched. Two flat timbers were laid upon the wall, and with ropes, the next log was rolled up the incline into position. All of the men were experienced timber men, and the axes and saws were kept in continuous motion. By the time noon came, the walls were nearly in place. As the men ate, Matt and Jane went with a piece of chalk and marked the windows and both doors. The biggest window faced the river. The smell of fresh lumber was heavy in the air, but Jane was no stranger to such things. Her father, Mr. Robinson, owned the local lumber yard. He brought three large windows and a pair of doors as his donation to the project.

Afternoon got the crew to the point where they were putting the last of the shingles onto the roof. These neighbors had done this work before, but it had been some time since they had worked together so hard. The ladies kept them all supplied with lemonade and water. By the time darkness closed in around them, there was little else to do aside from hanging doors and windows.

The next morning, a few men came back and, in two hours, had the new home so enclosed that not even a mosquito could get in. The town's mayor had an old skeleton key and with a small ceremony outside of the general store, presented Matt and Jane with the key to their new home.

Evening found the family putting furniture in the cabin. Between Wil and Mr. Robinson, the young couple had plenty of extra stuff to get them going. The general store gave them a cook stove at cost and told them that they could pay for it over time if they wanted to. One of the local stonemasons agreed to put up the fireplace sometime during the summer. For the time being, they had to haul drinking water from Wil's well.

One of the most important things had been totally overlooked. The sitting room or outhouse, still had to be built and a hole dug for it. By evening, that project was taken care of as well, and someone had even thrown in a Sears catalog.

With the addition of a couple of oil lamps, this cabin was home. Matt and Wil admired their hard work and reminded everyone that there would be quite a dance after the big wedding tomorrow. It was getting on toward dark, and Matt drove Jane home for the last time. After the wedding tomorrow, she would be his wife and have a new name. Matt was excited by the thoughts of his new life with Jane and vowed to be there for her no matter what. She kissed him lightly and put her hand behind his neck. The two sat for a while in the car resting after the days labor.

"Alright! Get in here, girl," roared Mr. Robinson laughing. "And you boy. Get on home. It's getting dark."

Matt laughed and drove off toward home and a plate of supper.

Chapter 18: The Wedding

Matt swung his legs out of his bunk, and the chill of the floor caught his attention. He looked out the window expecting to see a cold rainy morning, but it wasn't to be the case. The sky was a bright burning blue, and there was hardly a ripple on the river. The birds were singing all over the place.

Ma was in the kitchen, and you could have smelled the ham frying for miles. She turned to greet him, and Matt saw that she had a smile the size of Texas on her face. Even Wil, not usually prone to excessive humor this time of day, had a big grin on his face, too. Matt walked over and gave Ma a big hug. Then he hugged Wil, something he hadn't done very often. Wil seemed somewhat embarrassed, but regained his composure rapidly.

"I'm so hungry I could eat a horse." said Matt

"Funny you should say that," she said. "That's exactly what we're having for breakfast."

They all laughed and sat down to the table. There were fried potatoes and turnips, one of Matt's favorite meals, and a pan of grits. That was especially made for Wil, but Matt might give it one more try. If he kept at it long enough, he might even learn to like it, but he had serious doubts about that.

After the breakfast was done, the men grabbed their hats and headed to the barn to check on the stock. The barn was unusually quiet this morning. The cows always made a racket when they heard them coming. Today was a bit different, though. Matt walked over to the cows, and Brownie, the biggest one, was laying down, not at all like her usual behavior. He gave a quick look and walked around behind her. There in the straw lay the reason for her change in behavior. It was a beautiful bull calf. Wil didn't seem to be too surprised since he had arranged the breeding himself. They sat down for a minute and looked at the new resident. Not many things in farming made a person feel this way, but a new calf sure had a way of bringing out the child in a man. Wil reached down and stroked the calf's flank. It was a beauty and when old enough would be sold for breeding stock.

They finally finished their chores and went back into the cabin for coffee. Ma had already cleaned up the breakfast dishes and had some sweets on the table to go with their coffee. Matt looked over, and there was his suit hanging, all pressed, and a starched white shirt, too.

"Did you think to buy flowers?" asked Ma.

Matt's jaw must have dropped a foot. It felt as if all of the blood had left his face. Now here was an excellent reason to panic. He stepped toward the door. He was in a hurry to get to town to buy the flowers, and Ma was laughing loudly. She told him not to make a move, and she brought out the most beautiful bridal bouquet he had ever seen.

"Oh, Ma, I guess you've thought of everything."

Matt drove to town a bit more relaxed than he had been a while before. It seemed that everything was under control. All he had to do was show up and bring the ring. He couldn't forget that. He arrived at his office and checked the bulletin board for messages. Nothing there, so all was still in good shape. He unlocked the door and went inside. He was a bit shocked when he heard something in the back room. He thought for a minute that some old jack had gotten in to sleep off his whiskey. He walked cautiously toward the back and nearly had a heart attack when Jane ran right into him in the doorway. She had been there to check on the bulletin board, too. She wanted nothing to get into the way of their big day.

"Jane!"

Jane put her hand to her mouth and said, "Matthew Andrews, you scared me out of five years of good living."

She took a deep breath and turned on her heel and walked right out into the sunshine. Matt was left wondering what had happened. It dawned on him that he wasn't supposed to see the bride until it was time to get married. He looked out the small window and saw Jane walking home with a cute little step that he knew was done for him. She sure was pretty. He sat down to his desk to write some notes on his patients and couldn't quite get into the mood for it. He was much too preoccupied with the day. His thoughts turned back to Minneapolis and what life was like back there for him. He thought of how he could work from early morning to late in the evening, and when he tallied up the bills for the month, there was always a lot of money left over. He kept putting it in the bank, and the years kept going by. Nothing significant ever seemed to happen in his life, nothing that he could look back on as being momentous. All that happened was that years went by with nothing to show for them except money.

Since his hunting trip last fall, everything in his life had been turned upside down. There was never much money, and his clothes needed to be thrown away and replaced. His hair grew wild and long and he wore it tied up in back. He was even starting to talk like the people that he lived with. It was a kind of a backwoods slang and he liked the way it sounded. Everything about his life was now different, and he loved each and every day. When he found Jane, he counted himself as a lucky man. She was a beautiful woman, and it made him proud to have her on his arm.

The wedding was to be at 4:00 p.m., and some of the ladies were already busy setting up the tables. There were even some white paper decorations hanging in the trees, and some on the tables. The river was a bit higher than usual, so the rapids, usually quite noisy from the splashing water, were nearly silent. There was a small bandstand near the water where they had a dance every once in a while and one usually on the Fourth of July. The great boulders near the river formed a half circle, and that is where the preacher would marry them, like so many had done before. There was a new carpet delivered for the occasion, a fresh blanket of gold and red maple leaves covered the entire ground as far as they could see, and the river shimmered in the sunshine. It was warm, and the slight breeze out of the south was welcome.

Matt went to his new cabin by the river to make sure that everything was ready for his bride. There were colorful unlit candles around the home and a lot of fresh baked goods sitting on the table. Some of the ladies had purchased material and made a set of new curtains and that really made it look nice. The floors were swept and clean. Matt's new shotgun hung over the doorway as a sign that Wil had been there too. There was even a new curtain across the doorway to their bedroom. He was quite pleased with the friendship that the community had shown him. They had welcomed him as one of their own.

He got back into his car and finished the drive home. Wil sat down by the river, and Matt walked over to talk to him. There was a spot on the bench for him, so he made himself comfortable.

"You know, boy, you sure have brought some new life into the two of us. There was a time not long ago that neither the old woman nor I had much left to say. We'd do our work and go to sleep. That was about it for us, until I went up to the Roseau last fall. You came back here with me and gave us a new life. We're back to laughing like old times. We both thank you, Matt."

"It's my turn to say thanks. I never had much of a life in Minneapolis. I made a lot of money, and in the process, I lost track of what's important. Here on the river, I've found out that all of the money in the world can't buy what I have here, family and friends. I remember a saying from the Good Book that goes, 'What profit it a man if he gain the whole world and lose his soul,' or something like that. I guess it must have been written about me."

"You know, Matt, I'm getting on in years now, and I guess that I've had some good times, but the best of course was since I met Ma. She had a way of lifting me up when things turned sour."

"How old are you now?"

"Well I'd have to think on that a bit, but I do remember that when I was a kid, the Mississippi River only went about forty miles or so."

Matt laughed hard with Wil.

"You got me again."

They stood up, and Wil put his arm around Matt's shoulder. They walked quietly to the back door of the cabin.

When they came back in, they noticed a new aroma coming from

Ma's stove. She was in the process of making a wedding cake for Matt and Jane. It seemed that she couldn't do enough for her kid. They had taken in a stray, and it turned out to be the right thing to do. He had turned into their son, and they had turned back into parents again. Ma walked over and asked Matt if he was ready for the big day. He still had to take a bath and get dressed. Ma had hot water on the stove for him and had taken the big washtub into his room. They carried the hot water in along with a couple buckets of cold water, he was ready to indulge himself in a rare tub bath.

He washed his hair first and then on down to the tips of his toes. By the time that he got done, the water was nearly cold. By the way his hand was shaking, it was a tossup whether or not he would cut his own throat while he was shaving.

When he'd finished shaving, he looked over at his wedding suit. At the moment, he felt a bit nervous, hoping that all would go well this afternoon. Ma cut his hair a bit so it wouldn't be so straggly, and then he got dressed, ready for the big event. He put a dab of Brilliantine in his hair and some men's cologne on his neck. His freshly shaved face grinned back at him in the mirror.

It was nearly time, and Ma and Wil were all dressed up and ready to go. Wil stopped and got the wedding gift from their room and went to the car. Matt followed along behind them, and it seemed to him that they were driving way too fast to suit him. He was getting a bit more nervous as the time wound down.

They arrived at the Bigfork River nearly a quarter to the hour. He saw the preacher, the best man, the bridesmaid, Mr. Robinson, and over to the side a short way a young boy laying on the ground bleeding profusely. He ran over to him and saw that he had cut his hand nearly to the bone while trying to carve his initials into the picnic table. He scooped up the boy and ran across the street to his office. He again took a look at the boys hand and found that the cut had gone across all of the tendons, and unless he could get doctored up soon, the boy would lose most of the use of his hand.

He turned to the boy's Ma and told her to hold him so that he wouldn't fall off the table. He turned back to get the disinfectant and saw Jane hurrying in to help. She was dressed all in white like a nurse, but this time, it was her wedding dress. She knew what to do and got ready with some carbide lamps for light. She got the big magnifying glass out and set it up over the boy's hand. She draped the area in white towels and got the doctors tools ready for him.

Matt had been scrubbing and when he got done, he put on a white apron. He approached the patient and told the young boy that he would be fine in a few minutes. He injected the boy with a numbing agent and checked to see if the area was ready. By the light of the carbide lamps, Dr. Matt attempted to find the loose tendons and get them back in place. Each stitch was extremely small and had to be done with precision. The boy was cooperating by not moving, and Matt was coming to the last of the tendon work. Then, it was time to close. He sutured the cut with expertise and speed. In time, the patient was bandaged up with a large ball of white gauze. He got off the table and looked at his hand. After all of the excitement had subsided, the boy started to cry. He was making a tremendous fuss, and Matt had to ask what he was crying about. He wanted his new knife back, and that was all there was to it. His mother slapped his butt and told him to head for home. Matt and Jane looked at each other and laughed.

The wedding had been delayed a bit, but it was still going to take place. Matt looked in the mirror and combed his hair. Jane looked into the mirror and saw the blood splatters on her dress sleeve. She grabbed the scissors and cut off half of the sleeve and then did the other one.

She looked at Matt and said, "Ready?"

Matt took her arm, and they opened the door and walked outdoors toward the party. The crowd soon saw them and broke out in applause. Matt walked Jane over to her folks and went to see the preacher.

"You stand here," said the preacher.

The band tuned up a bit and played the wedding march. Jane and her dad walked toward the big rocks and the waiting groom to be. Mr. Robinson took Jane's hand and placed it in Matt's.

"Now, Jane," said the preacher, "this is the last chance to change your mind."

"Don't be telling her such nonsense," said Matt grinning. "I just got her talked into saying 'yes' only a few days ago."

The preacher said something about do you take this woman, and the next thing Matt knew, they were walking back toward the guests. It was done, and he had his best friend Jane as his wife. The entire community came up to congratulate the couple. They were led to the head table and sat down with their backs to the river. The music continued, and the food was passed around to all. It was time to cut the beautiful cake that Ma had made. The knife was laying beside the cake, and together they cut the first piece. Jane fed a small bite to Matt, and he did the same for her. The guests all clapped their hands.

After dinner, the dancing started. There were many polkas and waltzes, and at one time they even threw in a schottische to see if Matt knew how to do it. He surprised them all. Matt and Jane danced beautifully together way into the evening. When a friend of Matt's tried to cut in on them, Matt pretended not to hear or see him. It was all in fun, and the entire community said that they had never seen such a fun wedding.

It was nearing 10:00 p.m., and the oil lamps were fading out one by one as night claimed the river. Matt whispered to his wife and she nodded yes. The two stood up and thanked everyone for making this such a special day, then walked arm in arm to their car. Their nice shiny car had been fully decorated with many good wishes in white, and there were the usual cans and old shoes tied to the bumper.

The trip home went all too fast, and in short order they were nearing their new cabin. Both of them felt a bit nervous as they walked up to the door. Matt opened it and lit a lamp. He lifted his bride and carried her over the threshold. Once inside, he kissed her softly and said, "I love you, Mrs. Andrews."

Chapter 19: Office Hours

The next afternoon, the couple opened their gifts from the many friends, relatives, and neighbors. The very first to be opened was one wrapped in stunning white paper with white ribbons. Jane unwrapped it slowly and found a beautiful homemade blanket that Ma had sewn herself. She got up immediately and put it on their bed. It was all done in white with their names across the edge also sewn in white silk thread.

It was Matt's turn, and he opened one from Jane's folks. It was a new set of fireplace tools and some pots and pans, all things that they didn't have the money to buy yet. The whole community gave gifts of one kind or another. The entire day was spent at their new home, and when evening came, Matt brought out the bottle of champagne that he had bought from Jane the first day that he met her. They lifted their glasses in a toast to a long and happy life.

Life for Matt had taken a turn for the better. He had a woman in his life who was a sheer joy to be around. He awoke each morning to find a smiling wife looking back at him from the other side of the bed. Her pleasant demeanor followed her throughout the day and in all situations. The patients that came in to see them were always treated well and with kindness. Even the tough old lumberjacks liked having a pretty gal to talk to, but sometimes they stretched even her to the breaking point.

A crusty, old jack was brought in injured. The sawyers yelled timber, and the jack moved away from the falling tree, but a large branch clipped him solidly and knocked him to the ground. He lay there stunned for a while until the boss found him. He tried to help the man to his feet, but each time he tried, the jack crumpled in pain. The men rigged a stretcher for him and got him to the cook shack. By that time, he was bleeding from his mouth. The cook saw the blood. After a quick look, he said that they better get him to town to a real doctor. The men put him on the back of the truck and headed the ten miles to town to see Dr. Matt.

It was almost noon when Matt heard the horn blowing, and the truck pulled up to the office. He put down his sandwich and went out to see what had happened. He gave a quick look at the man and sent for Jane to help him. The men laid the jack on the table and went to leave.

"Don't leave me here. Whatcha gonna do to me?"

He was scared, and it didn't look good on a man as tough as he was.

"What happened?" asked Matt.

"Don't really know, but I tink da tree got me."

By that time, Jane had arrived and was trying to get his shirt off. He wasn't going to have any part of that in front of a lady, so Jane had to turn her back for a while. When she turned around, she noticed that the man was very hairy. On closer inspection she was horrified to find that he was wearing longhandles, and his body hair had grown right through the material. The man had a very bad odor, but she was used to that in some of the woodsmen. However, she had never seen anything like this before.

"Doctor? I think that I might need some help," said Jane.

Matt came over and saw the problem and handed Jane a pair of barber clippers.

"It looks like you're going to have to cut them off. I would guess that it's going to take a while, so I'll be out in the front office. There's a new baby coming in pretty soon."

Matt turned around and disappeared.

Jane was never one to shrink from a job, so she informed the jack of what she was going to do and took no guff from the man. Within a minute, he had the rest of his outer clothes off, and Jane had thrown them in the corner. Next, she dusted him with lice powder and sprayed him with a mild disinfectant. Then, she started the job. She clipped the back of his neck and cut off the smelly longhandle material as she freed it up. The patient by that time had resigned himself to the fact that he was going to get a shave, but he pleaded with Jane, never to tell anyone.

"Please, miss. Ya just can't tell da rest of da men. They'd give me sich a bad time. Please."

"Now sit still, Sven," Jane said. "I'm not exactly liking this job."

She got a serious look on her face. Sven tried to cover himself when Jane had her back turned to get a new clipper.

"Sven, you sit still there, or I'll send you back to camp just the way you sit."

"Oh, now, have a heart, miss."

When she got down to the more sensitive areas, she allowed him to finish the job. Jane scrubbed him up as much as she was allowed, and then the old jack had to finish the rest. Lye soap and a stiff scrub brush helped. Dr. Matt handed him a robe, and he sat down on the examination table.

"How long you been wearing them longhandles, Sven?"

"Well, Doc, I went to take dem tings off last summer, and I just can't do it, so I been wearing dem ever since. I didn't spect to get hurt, but I guess dats one way to get dem tings off me."

Matt had the man lay down on the table for an examination. He checked his heart and lungs and found them both to be in good condition. As he moved his stethoscope, he could hear bones grinding each time the man inhaled.

"Looks like you have a few broken ribs. I'm going to wrap you up tightly, and that will make breathing a bit easier for you. You come back and see me in a couple weeks. In the meantime, don't do any lifting, sawing, or swinging an axe."

The man asked what he could do, and Matt told him to do nothing until he saw him again. Matt told him that he would talk to the boss and see if there was any work that he could do in the cook shack for a while.

When it came to the end of the conversation, he asked where his clothes were. Matt found them and handed them to the man. He dropped them as if they were on fire.

"Fus dat shmell?"

Matt laughed hard and told the man that it was from his clothes. After an hour of breathing fresh air, he didn't much care for the odor.

"Could I ask ya to go get me some new duds?"

"I'm sure Jane would be glad to do that for you. Where is your money?"

Sven pointed at the pants on the floor, and Matt kicked them over to him. He retrieved a big wad of money and peeled off fifty dollars for new clothes. It was the first investment in clothing in some time.

Jane went next door to the general store and knew right off where the clothes for Sven would be found. She picked out a pair of four dollar pants and looked them over. She put them back and took down a pair that cost ten dollars. Then the shirt was selected. She picked out the most expensive one. Socks were next with a price tag of two dollars a pair. She took three pairs. Longhandles for most folk were a winter garment, but for the jacks, they used them all year. Two pairs would do. She added it all up, and including the suspenders, it came to twenty-four dollars. She thought to bring Sven the change, but she decided to spend the whole fifty dollars. She went back and bought more pants and shirts until it got to exactly fifty dillars. Satisfied with her purchase, she paid for the whole thing and brought the new clothes next door to Sven.

"How much did all dis schtuff come to?"

"Well, it took the whole fifty dollars, and I want you to change your clothes at least every Saturday night after you take a bath," Jane laughed. "You could do with a shave and a haircut too."

"Yup. I'm gonna get over to dat barber shop right after I'm done wit you. I might even get some of dat nice smelling schtuff for my hair. Den I'm going to da saloon."

Matt laughed and gave the man a bill for twenty dollars. Sven tried to walk out without paying, and Matt stood in his way blocking the door. The jack outweighed him by at least a hundred pounds, but in his condition, he figured that it might be better to pay. These were tough men, but they all liked Dr. Matt and wanted to stay friends with him. You never knew when you might need the services of the good doctor, so he dug deep into his new pockets and came up with a wad of money. He unrolled it and counted out twenty dollars.

"Tanks, doc." said the jack, and he headed out the door. "Oh ya. Dis is fer da missus," he said handing Matt some more cash. He walked out the door toward the barber shop.

He had given ten dollars to Jane, but Matt wasn't quite sure what it was for. Had he liked the way she treated him or was it perhaps bribery money so she wouldn't tell the rest of the crew about the shave?

That evening the newlyweds had company for dinner. Wil and Ma had come to see them and asked if they needed anything. Ma had a big smile, and Jane had one to match. She was very proud to show off her new house. She also was a good cook, but not to the degree that Ma was. That took a lot of years and hard times.

After the supper was over, Matt and Wil walked outside to talk.

"Are you going to be able to hunt this fall? It's only about a week until it's time to go."

"Absolutely, but I don't know if I can stay gone as long as before. It seems like we're getting new patients almost every day. I had asked a friend that I met this summer if he would take any emergency patients that came in for a week, and he said that he would. I'll contact him, but I guess that means that I can go for just a week. What do you think, Wil?"

"If you can only go for a week, how about going to Manitoba?"

"What would we hunt up there?"

"Well, I used to hunt for moose years back until they started to charge for a hunting license. Now you have to pay ten dollars for a week of hunting. I guess I could come up with that much."

Matt immediately got that old feeling again, the smell of gunpowder and the good earth raced through his mind. He thought of the time barely a year ago when he met his friend Wil. A lot of things had happened in that year, and they were all good things. His new wife, a new office, and most of all his newfound family. All of these were at the very top of his list. He felt like an extremely lucky man.

"When are we going to leave?"

"Well, I thought that we could leave on Friday after you get done.

That'd give me time to pack the trailer and all our stuff. We need a block and tackle and the usual stuff like axes and saws. If you never done this before, you got a lot to learn. What kind of a rifle are you going to use?"

Matt thought for a moment and remembered that he didn't own a rifle. He would go to the general store and see what they had.

"I guess I'll have to buy one. I don't suppose you know how much they are, do you?"

Wil looked at him and made another of those decisions that are better left to a husband and wife together. He had the boy's new 45-70 Government rifle, and it had never even been fired. He knew that Ma liked the idea. He and the boy had bought the gun when he was home and had never gotten the chance to use it.

"I've got one at the house that you can have. It's never been fired, and I'd be right pleased if you'd take it."

Again Matt knew what the old man was thinking about, and all he could say was thank you. There was a closeness between the two that felt a whole lot more like family with each passing day. It seemed, too, that there were a lot of things that didn't need to be said.

The next day, Wil and Matt got out the guns and did a little shooting to see if they could hit anything. Wil fired four shots and hit the tin can each time. It was Matt's turn to show his stuff. He fired, and the can never moved. He fired again and still nothing. Once more he gave it a try and came up empty. Wil stood by watching, and it seemed like Matt was flinching quite a bit.

"Dammit boy. You better stick to shotguns. You couldn't hit a moose in the ass with a bass fiddle. Hand me that gun for a minute."

Wil took the gun and looked it over from front to back and shouldered it to check the comb. Everything seemed good to him. He thought about the flinching that Matt was doing.

"Here, use one of my shells."

Wil opened the action and pretended to put in a cartridge. He closed it back up and told Matt to use the car hood for a rest.

"Now take a good aim and squeeze the trigger smoothly."

Matt tried to rest on the hood, but couldn't get a comfortable position. He decided to shoot offhand, with no rest at all. He brought the gun up again and sighted carefully. When he pulled the trigger, he flinched so badly that it nearly gave him a broken neck. He jumped like a bomb had gone off. There was one small difference; however, there was no accompanying noise. Wil had fooled him into giving away the nature of his problem. He was unconsciously afraid of the recoil and jerked the trigger even when he tried not to. That wasn't the first time Wil had seen it, and he knew what to do right away. Matt reloaded a single cartridge and aimed carefully. This time he was told to squeeze the trigger so gradually that he would have no idea when the gun was going to fire. He hit the target dead in the center and did it time after time. The gun was great, and Matt said that he would take good care of it. Wil grinned a bit as they drove back to the cabin.

Matt started to make a list of the things they needed, and for the next couple days, they stayed busy getting everything loaded. This time it was going to be a different trip. They needed the equipment to move a lot of heavy meat. Jane was as excited as Matt about the trip. She and Ma had made plans to take the train to International Falls to do some shopping. It was a good time for them all. The excitement built until Friday morning when the two ladies left town. Then, the men folk put the finishing touches on their load. Matt purchased a box of 180 grain shells, and Wil had a part box that he had been using out of for years. Ma sent several quarts of stew and soup so that they wouldn't die of hunger.

The afternoon found Dr. Matt back at work looking after a newborn baby. A sniffle had the new mom in a panic, and Matt had to treat her more than the baby. He gave her a peppermint stick and sent her back home for rest. New moms need a lot of rest and get very little. He was glad that the afternoon didn't require much thinking, because he couldn't have done it. His thoughts had turned to the hunt, and now it was time to hit the road.

He went back to Wil and Ma's place, and they hooked up the trailer. It wasn't loaded too heavy, because if they were successful, the meat would be more than enough weight. Jane had left some cookies in a bag on the car seat, and that made both of them smile. Trips like this weren't enough to get Wil's heart beating fast, but Matt's was in high gear as they pulled out, headed for Canada.

Chapter 20: Manitoba

The trip north had put both men in good spirits. As they neared the border crossing, they stopped to check their load and filled the car up with gasoline. Matt came back to the car with two sacks of peanuts and a bottle of Coca-Cola for each of them. He opened the bag and carefully poured them into his bottle. Wil stared at him as if he had lost some of his mind.

"What did you just do with them peanuts?"

"I learned that back in medical school from some of those kids from the south. We never had time to eat between classes so we made the most of a bad situation and killed two birds with one stone."

Wil shook his head and ate his in what he considered to be a more normal fashion. Sometimes these young kids really surprised him.

After they crossed the border into Canada, the roads got dramatically worse, and Wil had to rely on memory to get to the spot he had hunted a few years back. Roads change, and the countryside changes, but north is still north, and the lakes and rivers were right where he left them. By the time night fell, they were close to their destination. Pulling off the road and going down a logging road for several miles got them near to where he wanted to be. In the night, the trees seemed to hang further over the road and made it feel like driving through a tunnel. There was a covering of wet leaves on the road and that made for some hazardous driving. Wil pointed to his left and there was what looked like a small clearing a short way from the gravel road. He turned in and shut off the car. Matt dug out a kerosene lantern, lighting up the area so they could get settled in for the night. It was getting late, and they were both dog tired. The cold wind and frost made them glad that they had a tent. In very short order, it was put up, and they had settled their bones for the night.

Morning, as always, found Wil to be the first one up and the campfire was going strong. The coffee bubbled and hissed and was nearly done. Wil took it from the fire and poured some cold water into the pot to settle the grounds. He poured a cup and sat back on a log to look around. The sky was getting a bit lighter in the east, but in the west, there was still a sky full of sparklers. He saw the Big Dipper and followed the end two stars in the cup off to the north star, right where he had left it the last time he was here. The stars winked out one by one, and he truly enjoyed sitting there watching the world go by. He had always appreciated God's handiwork and marveled at its beauty.

"You got that coffee done?" said Matt from inside the tent.

"You may not be able to shoot, but you can sure find the coffee."

In a while, Matt had dressed and came out to greet the rising sun. Today was a day of rest and scouting for them. This was new territory for Matt, and he needed to learn a bit more about it. He had bought a compass and hoped that he wouldn't need it. He dug out his binoculars to be used today for spotting. He was excited and had a hard time sitting still until the frost burned off.

The camp was made ready, and there were two trees nearby that had a long piece of pipe hung between them, something that Wil had left the last time he was here. It was a good place to hang meat and offered a bit of shade to keep it cool. There was some small brush that had grown up since his last hunt, and Matt chopped it off even with the ground so that nobody tripped. There wasn't much firewood around, so they decided to make that the first chore of the day. This time, there was no two-man saw, so they took out the bow saws and cut down a couple dead trees for the fire. Within an hour or two, the wood was hauled back to camp, split, and stacked near the fire. The empty trailer made short work of a hard job.

Matt poured another cup of coffee for them both, and they sat for a moment to catch their breath. He noticed that Wil was breathing a bit heavier than he had seen before, but he didn't think too much of it. They decided to walk down the gravel road a ways and look for tracks where the moose had been crossing. The sumac brush in the area was a splendid red, and the leaves that were left on the birch trees gave a golden shine to the whole area. The wind, however, was brisk, and the two men were glad for their warm clothes.

In about a mile they had counted at least fifteen sets of tracks of shooting size animals. Wil mentioned a beaver dam that was a quarter mile back in the woods, and the two headed toward it. They had no more than stepped into the tree line when they heard an animal crashing brush right in front of them. Both men were alert now, staring toward the noise. You never knew what to expect from a moose. They could either run away or run right over you. Wil's hand dropped down to his pistol without even thinking. The noise went away, and the men walked back out to the road.

"I would say that it might be a good idea for you to be here around daylight tomorrow," said Wil. "Moose are creatures of habit, and I'll bet that sometime during the day tomorrow, you'll see one right near that pond."

"Where will you be?"

"I think that I'll head back down the other direction from camp, where we got our firewood. There was a lot of red willow there, and that's about the best spot to find them in midday. Besides, I'm not too sure where your bullets will fly."

They both laughed. He was still kidding Matt about his flinching problem. They scouted out several areas and had it narrowed down to a couple that looked the best.

As the sun got close to the trees, the two men walked slowly back down the road toward camp. It was time to get some kind of food put together for dinner. Wil said that it was Matt's turn to cook, and Matt figured that he could handle a small job like that.

The first thing Matt did was to dig out his big cast iron frying pan. It had a layer of grease burned to the outside of it, but the inside was clean as a whistle. He placed it on the grate and stirred up the coals. He took some butter out of a can and started to cut up some onions, several onions. He tended them with care, and when they had turned a perfect brown, he poured them out onto a large plate. They smelled excellent. If dinner didn't go any further tonight, the onions would be enough to keep them both happy. Matt put the skillet back on the campfire and let it get good and hot. He reached behind him into his wooden food locker and retrieved two large beef steaks wrapped in white butcher paper. He held them up for Wil's inspection.

"Now where did you get those?" asked Wil.

"Well, before we left home, Jane put them in the food locker, along with a couple other things, with orders that we should eat them as soon as we made camp. She takes darned good care of me even when she's not here. She's a terrific woman!"

Matt put the steaks in the pan, and they began to sizzle loudly. He threw two big potatoes into the coals and sat back to enjoy the show. In a short time, the potatoes popped and steam started to escape from them. He turned the steaks over to reveal one side that was beautifully browned. He turned the potatoes with a stick, and they looked pretty black on the bottom. Then it was time to throw the onions back onto the steaks. They sizzled as they hit the pan. Wil sat there silently waiting for his meal, enjoying the aroma. He made no offer to help, and Matt asked for none. He had it all under control.

Within a few short minutes, the steaks were removed from the fire and set aside to rest. Matt busied himself getting a couple of plates ready for the meal. Then he went back into his locker and retrieved a small unlabeled jar. He scooped out a generous amount of homemade horseradish and put it on his plate.

"Got any of that for an old man?"

"You bet I do," said the cook.

Wil put a big scoop on the side of his plate and stood there like a beggar holding his cup. Matt took a pair of sticks and dug out the spuds. He brushed off the ash and cut them open with his knife. On each steaming potato, he put a big hunk of butter. His attention turned to the frying pan. He took a long handled fork and served a steak up onto each plate. The result of his efforts nearly equaled the goose that Wil cooked last year. He took the remainder of the onions and divided them up between the two plates. Wil looked at the meal and wondered if he could eat it all. He'd give it his best try.

Chapter 21: Wolves

The evening dishes were cleaned up, and neither wanted to move very far from the campfire. It seemed to Wil that the food tasted better in a hunting camp. After the meal of steak and potatoes, Matt surprised Wil again with a jar of sugar sweetened strawberries. He wasn't able to eat his share and didn't even have room for coffee. Jane had sent along enough to feed four people.

The moon came out, and a cool breeze worked its way through the camp. It was late fall, and snow couldn't be far off. It felt as if it could snow any time, but Wil's knee made no such announcement.

From quite a way off, they heard the call of a single wolf. No others joined in, so it meant that he was a loner and not inclined to be hunting that night. Wolves usually roamed the countryside in groups of six to ten. There was only one female that would breed, and only one male that sired pups. The only time that you saw a lone wolf was when he had been dethroned by a young upstart, one much stronger than himself and usually much younger. The old king lived out the remaining days of his life hunting mice and voles for his dinner, not at all like the moose and deer that he had been accustomed to.

"Did you hear that wolf, Matt? It makes me think of a time when I was just a kid. I had to spend a night alone in the woods.

I was just barely eleven years old, and my dad had just given me my own gun. I had hunted before when we put up meat for the winter, but this time I went out on my own. I walked out across the road from the cabin to a spot where I'd seen deer feeding before. I just started hunting when a nice doe jumped up and headed for cover. I pulled up the gun and drew back the hammer. I concentrated hard on the running deer and squeezed the trigger. The deer's tail dropped but she kept on running. I stopped and waited for a half hour like I was taught, then walked over to where she was last seen. There was quite a bit of blood high on the bushes, and it was frothy pink which meant a lung shot. In any case, the deer was still moving, and I had to retrieve it. Nobody left an animal to die in the woods to be wasted. This was food needed for our family.

I looked hard and found a good solid blood trail and followed it slowly, being careful not to miss anything. It was only a matter of a few minutes, and I jumped her again in a swampy area. She made a lot of noise this time as she went through the brush. When I got to where she jumped up, I could see that she'd been laying down but not bleeding very much. The whole story was there on the ground for the reading. As I started trailing her again,I noticed that the blood trail was drying up.

I got right down on the ground so I could see the tiny flecks of blood on the leaves, and at times I lost the trail completely. When that happened, I looked around and asked myself which way I would go if I were tired and weak and looking for a place to hide. The answer this time was downhill and toward cover.

I looked ahead and found such an area leading down to a small pond. I had only gone a couple hundred yards when I found flecks of blood about knee high on some dead fern leaves. This time the blood was very wet and still bright pink. I didn't think that she'd be too far ahead.

I trailed the wounded animal for another four hours and wasn't able to get close enough for a shot. When the opportunity presented itself, I was caught off guard and had to make a quick shot through light brush. The doe went down and didn't move. I made a bad shot, and the deer suffered for a long time before I could finish the job. My father wouldn't have thought too much of this.

I rolled the deer on its side and started to gut it out. The first cut told me that the deer had been bleeding inside for quite a while. I took some dried grass and wiped out most of the blood. Then, I put a rope around its neck and looked up to see which direction to head home. The sun had set, and the sky was dark with snow clouds. I didn't have any idea which direction to go, and it was getting dark. I wondered what my folks were thinking.

The very first thing I had to do was to make a fire. I got a small one going and started to gather firewood from as far away as the light of the fire let me see. I built it up a bit and gathered more wood. I figured that it might take quite a bit to last through the night. It turned cold, and I started to feel the effects of being drenched in sweat. I was cooling down and had to get warm or die of exposure. I built up the fire and took off my outer clothes down to my underwear and hung everything in the bushes to dry. It turned out to be a good plan, and within very few minutes, I had dry clothes again. A small amount of time spent shivering had saved me from certain death.

That night my entire world was defined by what the light allowed. It was about twenty feet around and dropped of like a black curtain. There weren't even any stars to help with directions.

Sometime later I tried to sleep. I gathered some grass and ferns to cover my back and faced the fire. I couldn't get to sleep, and in time, I saw something that scared me. I knew it was the wolves. There were eyes on the fringes of the firelight. They turned off and on, and then changed places. I didn't dare move, hoping that whatever it was would go away. I figured that their interest was in the fresh deer, but I wasn't sure. One of the pack tried to move in quickly for a bite of venison, and I threw a burning stick at him. He slowly moved back into the shadows.

After several hours, I saw the sky starting to lighten in the east and felt a little better. The clouds opened for a moment, and I got a quick look at the north star. I marked it in my head, and cut a line toward the river. I sighted from one tree to another to keep on a straight course and within an hour, I heard the rumble of the rapids. I had made it and knew exactly where I was. After another mile, I dragged the deer into the yard and walked into the cabin. Ma was cooking oatmeal for breakfast, and I was starving. She looked at me with tears in her eyes.

'Hungry?' she asked.

I never forgot that in all my years on the river. My folks didn't want anyone to know that they were worried."

Chapter 22: The Bull

Wil's thoughts came back to the here and now, and he noticed that the clouds were starting to drop a little snow on the ground. This was exactly what he wanted for the first day of his hunt, tracking snow. He didn't want very much, but if they could get an inch or two, it meant moose muzzle for supper. They both turned in early.

The next morning Wil took a quick look outside the tent and saw a light covering of snow on the ground. He got what he had wanted. He threw a few pieces of dry wood on the fire and in short order had a nice fire going and coffee in the pot. This was going to be a good day for a hunt and hopefully a chance for Matt to get his first moose.

They ate a hurried breakfast of sausage and eggs and got ready to head out to the areas scouted the day before. Wil put a biscuit in his pocket and his rifle over his shoulder and walked away into the darkness. Matt did nearly the same and walked down the road for quite a distance, watching for fresh tracks crossing the road. He saw none and entered the woods walking toward the beaver dam. The place he found had a view of a small pond a short distance away. As the sun started to lighten the clouds, he saw two beavers moving back and forth on the water.

Matt thought of a time a few years back when he lived near a small pond. He was in medical school. His desk at home was near a window that faced the lake. All summer he and his roommate watched the beavers gather browse and pile it near their lodge. There was a family of five beaver.

Summer turned to fall, and their gathering took on a more frantic pace. They could be seen at all hours of the day and night working. Finally, winter came, and the pond froze up. The temperatures in January and February were some of the coldest on record. Matt walked out to the lodge one day in late March and listened to see if he could hear any new additions to the family. He heard none.

Spring eventually came and with it a complete melting of the little pond. Ducks and geese were nesting and the whole place was alive. He watched intermittently to see how many beaver there would be but he never saw any. After four weeks there was still no activity.

One evening Matt and his roommate decided to open the lodge and see if there was any activity. The next morning they paddled the canoe out to the lodge and commenced to open it up. They struggled to take one piece at a time off, but each piece was intertwined with another. Several hours later, they had opened it enough to look inside. The smell was nearly overpowering.

Matt turned on his flashlight and was surprised to see the lodge floor littered with the corpses of the entire family of beaver. Sitting on the floor in the middle was a ball. It was the size of a baseball, and it was solid wood. It was chewed into a perfect sphere.

Matt's scientific mind unrolled the entire scene. The winter weather had frozen the waterway to their feeders and they couldn't get out. The last thing they tried was to chew on the timber of the lodge itself. With no nutrition in that, they all starved to death, hardly a fitting death for such an industrious neighbor.

The birds started to move around some, and a gray jay flew toward Matt on silent wings. Some called him the camp robber, but he was so pretty that Matt wouldn't think to say that about him.

With sunrise the cold deepened, but it didn't bother him too much. He was dressed warmly and had new rubber boots to keep dry. Then, the chickadees came looking for a handout. Matt held a piece of biscuit in his hand, and the small birds came in and dined in a nice warm place, the palm of his hand. They kept him entertained for quite a while searching for the small treasures that Matt brought out for them.

His perch on the incline of a broken tree top wasn't exactly comfortable, but he had seen worse. The show put on by the critters kept him wondering what he would see next.

A squirrel, out looking for some of the season's last acorns, stepped up onto his log and loped cautiously toward him. As he got within three feet of Matt, he stood up on his hind legs to get a better look. Panic set in when he realized how close he was to the stranger, and one small paw went up, crossed his chest, and rested over his heart. It looked to Matt as if this old gray fellow was having a heart attack. He had trouble keeping his voice down, but he did manage to laugh a bit, and the squirrel scampered off to view him from a much safer and healthier vantage point.

The day wore on to 3:00 p.m., and Matt's back side was sore from such an uncomfortable perch. He tried to move a bit, but his sleeping legs let him down, and none too gracefully. He landed on the snowy ground three feet below on his back. He lay still for a bit, taking inventory of his body parts until he was sure that nothing was broken. His circulation was coming back, and he tried to stand by grabbing onto a small tree. He was holding himself upright, trying to get some feeling in his feet, when he heard something splash water. He looked up to see a large bull moose walking into the water on the far side of the pond. His view of the animal was partly obscured with brush, so he just watched. The moose put his head down into the water and came up with a mouthful of green moss. The cold water didn't seem to bother him. Matt had thought for a moment of taking a shot while the animal had his head down in the water, but the thought of moving the moose out of the pond bothered him. He watched intently as the moose moved around finding the best feed for his huge body. He started to walk straight toward Matt and came up out of the water. He looked back over his shoulder at the two beaver and turned again toward Matt. Matt brought the rifle to his shoulder.

Squeeze the trigger, he thought to himself, and the rifle fired.

Smoke filled the air, and through it, he saw the big moose rear up high on his hind legs and turn back to where he had come from. He went only a few steps and fell down into the water. Matt was shaking all over from the excitement. He hoped the moose wouldn't get up.

After a few minutes of watching, he realized what kind of a predicament he had gotten himself into. The moose lay in about three feet of water, and there were no trees close enough to hook a block and tackle to. He decided to get Wil for some much needed help. When he got back to the road, he saw Wil heading toward him but still a long way off. He walked toward Wil, and when they met, Matt had a lot to say.

"I got one, Wil, and he's a big one, too. His rack must be six feet wide. We have a problem though. He's in the water, and I don't know how we'll move him."

Wil followed Matt in toward the beaver pond and found the big bull exactly as described. It was indeed a huge animal.

"What do you think we should do?"

"From where I stand, we have two choices. You can wade into the water and haul it back to camp in pieces, or we can build a fire and eat it right here."

"I guess we better get back to camp and get the saws and axes."

"Better get some rope, too."

They headed back to camp and got the car and trailer, bringing it to within a few hundred yards of the moose. The hunting rifles were left in the car, and the men headed to the pond.

"Now that is a real moose! I've seen them that big before, but I never thought that I could handle one that size."

Matt looked at the big animal and knew that he had stepped in it again. Wil was trying to be kind to him, but they both knew that this was a big job they had taken on. Matt walked into the water and touched the big bull on the nose. He didn't quite know where to start. Wil told him to gut it out first, so Matt started by reaching under water and cut the belly open. After a few swipes with the knife, that job was done. He had wanted to save the hide in one piece, but it couldn't be done. Next, he tied the rope around the head and threw the other end to Wil. He took the saw and cut it off, leaving Wil to haul it out of the water. It was too heavy for one, so the two men got on the rope and hauled it ashore.

"There, Matt, is our supper."

Matt looked and didn't see anything that he called food, but from past experience, he knew that he might just miss something once in a while.

"Moose muzzle."

"Now what in the world is that?"

"See that big nose? Well, that's moose muzzle, and it's great fried with onions."

Matt figured that he was going to eat some whether he wanted it or not, so he might just as well get used to the idea. Besides that, there were no more steaks to fry up.

"Put a rope around that left front leg and try to run the saw down the neck to the middle."

Half an hour later, they were both pulling on the rope trying to retrieve the prize. It slid out of the water with great effort and onto the shore. The whole quarter was picked up and laid on top of a couple logs. They ran a rope through the middle and hung it from a long pole. Each man put the pole to his shoulder and walked toward the car. By the time that they arrived, the previously frozen Matt was puffing and sweating profusely.

"How many more quarters are there in a moose?" Matt asked laughing.

"Enough to keep us in meat for the rest of the winter, I'd guess."

He was right, too. There was enough meat here for their needs, and shooting another was a waste of game. They would get the meat back to camp and decide from there what to do with it. Night had overtaken them as they got the first quarter hung on the meat pole. There was no chance to get back for another one before dark. They decided to call it a night.

"You get the frying pan, and I'll slice up the moose muzzle," Wil said. "I don't know if we've got any onions or not, but I do have some bacon to start it with. How about you getting a couple potatoes going again like last night."

Wil threw some more wood on the fire and went to cut up the hairy piece of moose nose. Matt watched him skin it and cut it in chunks. From there, he sliced it up into half inch slices and threw it in the pan. It looked alright so far. Wil threw in an onion and bacon and put it over the fire. It only took a moment for the onions to start smelling good, so in short order, Matt was introduced to one of the backwoods finest meals.

Dinner was eaten with few comments, and Matt did enjoy his

first try at moose nose. It was still early when they had things cleaned up, so Matt brought out a bottle that he had hid in the car. It was some kind of sherry, and they both took a cup full of it. It seemed to be what the doctor ordered, and Wil raised his cup in a toast to a successful hunt.

"I sure miss hunting the birds this year," said Wil. "There's a pile of them out on the river now, but I'm getting so that I don't much care to go alone."

"How about we go when we get back? I bought those two Chesapeakes, and they're getting pretty well trained. The northern flights have started, but no winter storms have pushed the big flocks through yet."

"I think that you'll have a couple days of your vacation left anyway. What do you say we head up Hay Creek off the river and camp for a couple days? I know a good place called the Lost Forty, and it's got a pretty good place to set a camp."

"Sounds like a good idea to me. I'm still trying to figure out how we can get the rest of that moose out of the woods, though."

"Well, it'll take us most of tomorrow, but then we can head south again. This has been a pretty fast hunt."

The next day they slept in for a bit because there was no reason to hurry daylight. They ate a big breakfast of bacon and flapjacks and sat for a second cup of coffee. Wil started to clean up the dishes, but Matt took over the job and had it done in no time. Wil looked pretty tired this morning and wasn't as full of laughter as usual.

They drove the car to the same place they had parked yesterday. When they got close to the pond, they heard a bit of cracking brush, and all was quiet. When they got to the pond, they saw the reason for the sound. Wolves had been eating on the moose head, and about all that was left was the rack and even that was chewed on some. They got to work quickly, and Matt sawed the rest of the front quarter from the carcass. After a hard pull, it was out, and the same routine took them back to the trailer. Then came a bit of harder work. The rest of the carcass was entirely under water, and Matt had to saw it down the middle to have any chance of getting it out. This required that he tie ropes around both the hind legs and try to turn him around and get him into the shallower water. Both men were exhausted by the time they'd accomplished that.

Matt made quick work of splitting the hind quarters, and in a few minutes, they had both quarters out on the bank of the pond. The same method was used to get the meat to the trailer, and then it was time to go to camp and wrap the meat for the ride home.

Wil had packed a new box of cheesecloth, and while the quarters hung on the meat pole, they wrapped them carefully so they stayed clean and the meat could breath for curing. Some of the meat had to be cut away to remove the gravel from the pond, but altogether there was plenty of meat for both families. The tent was packed, and the final cup of coffee was poured. Home wasn't that far away, and both men were eager to hit the road south.

Chapter 23: Hay Creek

The trip home was pretty uneventful, except for the border police wanting them to empty out the entire car and trailer before they could cross. They caught a couple of old ladies with a whole car full of illegal whiskey, so now they were checking every car. Also, the United States was in a serious war with Japan, and they didn't want any spies entering the country. One of them asked how big they thought the moose was, and Wil said that it was over half a ton.

They pulled into Wil's cabin about supper time, and Ma came out all full of smiles at their early return.

"Hello, darlin,'" Wil said. "Bet you're surprised to see us home this early."

"I am, but it sure is good to see. I already got to missing you."

That made it doubly hard to tell her.

"Actually, Ma, we're going out again tomorrow morning for ducks on Hay Creek."

"Wil Morgan, you know that you could shoot all the ducks you want right here on the river bank."

She was only kidding, and Wil knew that. There were some things that men just had to do.

Matt heard a shout. His bride was running through the woods. She had heard a car pull in and knew that it had to be them. She ran to Matt and put her arms around him, hugging him fiercely.

"It's not right you leaving me here alone when we just got married. Next time, I'm coming along."

"Well, you better get packed. We're leaving tomorrow morning to go up river for ducks."

The smile left Jane's face, but only for a moment.

"You still have a couple days left of your vacation, so you better use them if you can."

Again, her gentle spirit took over.

Jane looked at Ma and said, "How many ducks do you eat in a

141

year?"

"Well, I would guess that it's somewhere around twenty."

"And how many ducks do you have put up already?"

"Oh somewhere around thirty. You know, Jane, they could just as well stay home. I need the kitchen painted anyway."

They all laughed together.

"We won't be gone for long," Wil said.

Ma asked, "How did you two do this year anyway? We haven't had a good moose steak since last winter."

"Matt got a big one on the first day out, and we spent the rest of the time trying to get it back to camp."

They worked together and got all the meat hung in the root cellar for curing. It was always cool in there and never froze no matter how cold it got outside. Wil had dug it out of a hillside several years before and each year he put new grass and dirt on top of it. It was one of those things that people had to have in this part of the world.

Matt and Jane got into the car and headed back home. She knew he wouldn't be there long, but she'd cook him a good meal to make him come home for more. She had a hold of his arm and wasn't going to let go until she absolutely had to. They walked into the cabin, and Matt started to notice a few changes. There were knickknacks hung around the house, and in the bedroom, there was a new bedspread. The whole place had changed from when he left, and it was beautiful. The ladies had bought many nice things on their trip, and the cabin had been changed significantly.

She started to cook a meal, and Matt felt like he hadn't eaten in quite a while. There was corned beef and cabbage and a wild rice hot dish. The lady of this house was a terrific cook.

Next morning after chores and breakfast, Wil put his gear into the canoe and paddled down to get Matt. He was waiting there with his two Chesapeakes, Buck and Sam, and associated camping supplies. By the time that the canoe was packed, there wasn't much room for the hunters. The dogs were well behaved and whimpered a bit each time a duck jumped up. They were anxious for the hunt, too.

Hay Creek was only about four miles from Wil's cabin. The sun was shining, and it was quite a bit colder than it had been so far this season. Their wet hands chilled quickly and that made for some painful paddling, but both men kept up a steady stroke that ate up the distance. A turn north off the river got them into Hay Creek, and it felt like the current was against them. Neither man said much, and the canoe was dead silent in the water. Matt was in front, and when he raised his head for a moment's quick look, a nice buck raised his head at the same time. He was drinking water from the creek around a small bend. His big white tail went up, and he splashed hard in the boggy grass and disappeared throwing a fine mist of water up behind him. Matt was quite amazed at the power of the big animal. Neither of the dogs made much of a fuss since that critter didn't look much like a duck anyway.

They paddled a short distance more and had to lift the canoe over a small beaver dam. Not generally much of a task, today it was a hard job. The dogs got out first, and the men unloaded the canoe. They hauled it up and over the dam and reloaded it. Back on the creek, they continued paddling. The scenery was fantastic, and they kept jumping small flocks of curly tailed northern mallards. It had the appearance of another good shoot. One more beaver dam, and they would be getting close to the Lost Forty. In a short while, Wil nodded toward the shore, and they pulled in close enough for Wil to get out and steady the canoe for Matt. The dogs ran around for a while, getting rid of some of their pent up energies.

Setting up their camp wasn't much of a job since they were going to stay just one night. The tent and blankets were first out to keep them dry. A small wooden box with their food was set into the tent to keep the dogs out of it. Wil built a quick fire and started a pot of coffee. The sky was starting to darken some.

"Do you feel up to doing some jump shooting, Matt?"

"I sure do, and I'll do the paddling."

"Nope. I'll paddle. I need the exercise anyway."

Matt grabbed his shotgun and headed for the canoe. Wil paddled, and Matt took a crack at anything that jumped up in range. Buck and Sam were pretty well behaved, but when the gun went off, they nearly panicked. The mallards were thick on the creek, and once in a while one fell in the tall grass. Matt sent the dogs after them, and in a short while, they came back with their prize. Wil turned the canoe around when it started to get dark. They had six nice fat mallards. One more good shot before they got back to camp made it a total of seven. These northern mallards were large ducks, and it only took one for a good meal.

Wil paddled the canoe to the camp, and Matt pulled it up on solid ground. They dragged it up a ways closer to the tent and tipped it over to be used for a shelter for the dogs. Wil's fire was almost out, so he added a bit of wood to it and told Matt to get the food box out. He first located the frying pan and set it on the fire. He went into the box to take out the jar of stew that Ma had sent with them. Supper was pretty fast this night, and in no time, they were eating Ma's cooking and fresh bread. The coffee was again made from swampy tasting Hay Creek water, but neither of them complained too much. In all of Wil's travels, this was his favorite place. The smoke from the small fire curled upwards and disappeared into the balsam branches. The stars were so bright that you could almost hear them and off to the north. Upstream from camp, there was a small opening in the tree line. There, you could see the flashing and gyrating of the northern lights. They moved from left to right and then jumped high only to fade and come back somewhere else. It was a beautiful show, and one not seen by many.

They talked for a while about ducks and hunting and decided to call it a day early. There were decoys to load tomorrow and Buck and Sam to be taken care of. They knew that the hunting would be good from the small sample tonight. Sleep came easily for them, and soon the sounds of slumbering men and dogs was all there was to break the silence.

"Did you hear that?" Wil whispered.

"Whhhh what?" Matt said sleepily.

"A real big flock of geese just came over and landed on the creek not very far from here. We'll get them in the morning."

When it started to get light, Wil tied the dogs to a tree, and the men got into the canoe. They drifted slowly down stream using the paddles only when they had to straighten out the canoe. The geese were still there, but it sounded like they had drifted quite a way down stream. They paddled a bit and went to drifting again. Wil was worried that the geese might get up to leave as it got lighter. These geese were in full migration, and only stopped to feed when they had to. In the half light, they saw the flock and ducked down in the canoe. They were right in the middle of the flock when Wil whispered.

"Now!"

They raised up as the entire flock did, and when the shots went off, three geese hit the water. They reloaded quickly and knocked two more down. Matt's heart was beating wildly. He had never done anything like this before, and the excitement to him was nearly overwhelming.

They sat there in the canoe for several minutes, watching the rest of the geese gain altitude and wing southward. Matt paddled around as Wil picked them up. They had taken six geese, and that made for many good winter meals.

They paddled back to camp and pulled up onto shore. The sight that greeted them was like nothing either of them had seen before. The tent was torn down and ripped in many places. The food locker was broken in pieces and further over, he saw what remained of their dogs. They were still by the tree they were tied to, but all that remained of Buck was his head, and Sam was dead too, from a broken neck. Wil shook his head and looked at Matt.

"It's my fault," Wil said. "I would have bet anything that the bears were denned up by now."

"It's not your fault, Wil. Bears are pretty unpredictable. Do you want to go after him?"

"I'd like to, but I guess I don't have the stomach for it now. Besides, we'd never catch up with him."

The old man got a terribly angry look on his face and he showed it in his eyes. He went over to the fire and sat down to heat some coffee. There wasn't much that could be said at the time so Matt sat down with him.

"I had them tied to a tree, and they couldn't get away from that bear. He walked into camp and had the run of the place."

Chapter 24: Goin' Home

They put what remained of their gear into the canoe and before they left, they dug a shallow pit and buried what was left of Buck and Sam. They covered the makeshift grave with rocks and left the spot to the critters of Hay Creek. Matt was thinking that he might never want to come back here, but Wil said that it was part of what made Minnesota the wild place that he loved.

They drowned the fire and got into the canoe. It was a lot easier to paddle with so much less gear, and they were going downstream to boot. Even the beaver dams were easier. They saw them coming up and paddled hard to jump them landing with a great splash on the downstream side. Matt told Wil that he paddled pretty good for an old guy, and Wil never even looked around at him. That had the doctor in him a bit worried.

They made it to the river again and paddled to Wil's place. Matt pulled the canoe up on the shore a short distance and tipped it over. Their ducks and geese had to wait until the morning to be cleaned. They walked to the house carrying their guns, and Ma welcomed them inside. The old man took off his hat and coat and sat down in his rocker. She looked at her husband and asked him if he was alright. He briefly told her of their trip and accepted a cup of tea. Matt sat with them for a while watching Wil's face for anything that might tell him what was wrong. His color was off, but Matt didn't want to make too much of it. He took Wil's wrist and felt his pulse. It was high, but that could have been the strain of the paddling.

"I have to go home, Wil. There's a really pretty lady waiting to see my whiskered face. Thanks for another good trip."

He got up to go and motioned for Ma to walk him to the door.

"Wil didn't seem to be himself the last few days. Has he had any problems with his health?"

"No, he seemed fine to me, just as spry as ever."

"It seems like there is something wrong, and I'd like to see him in my office tomorrow early. I'll pick him up and bring him back."

Ma had a worried look on her face, and she kissed Matt on the cheek.

"Thanks."

That morning there was still snow in the air from the night before. It looked a lot like winter had hit the Bigfork valley. Everything was covered with a fresh coat of four inches of white.

Matt drove into Wil's yard and walked in. Wil was grinning from one ear to the other. He asked Matt in and poured him a cup of coffee. He seemed to be in much better condition than yesterday. Wil explained to him that sometimes things like that happen, and that was all there was to it. He felt fine now.

Matt thought for a while and insisted that Wil come to the clinic if for no other reason than to make the good doctor feel better. There was a reason for the poor color in Wil's face and his shortness of breath. Ma agreed, and Wil felt rather outnumbered.

Matt hadn't eaten breakfast yet, so he pulled up a chair. There was the usual meal on the table, meat and fried potatoes and a pot of oatmeal. The formality of waiting to be asked had gone by the wayside many months ago.

"All set for your big examination, Wil?"

"About as ready as an old goat like me can get," he grinned weakly.

"It shouldn't take much more than a few minutes, and we'll be back for the second cup of coffee. You know something, Wil? I never even liked coffee until I met you. See what you've done to me?"

They drove to the office and walked inside.

"This is a nice place. I helped build it, but I haven't seen much of it. This is only the second time I have ever been seen by a doc in my life."

"Here, get up on the table and lift your shirt."

He took out his stethoscope and listened carefully.

"Any thing in there?"

"Shhhhhhh. Take a deep breath and let it out slowly."

Matt listened carefully and thought that he heard a bit of trouble with Wil's heart. There was an unusual squishing sound, and that meant a problem with his aortic valve. He could also hear a strong murmur.

"Lay down here on your back, Wil."

He listened again for the sound that he had heard earlier. There it was again, along the left sternal border. He helped Wil up and handed him his shirt.

"It sounds like you're having some trouble with your old ticker, Wil. I'm going to give you some medicine. It's made from foxglove flowers."

Wil chuckled and said that maybe it was a bit premature to give him flowers.

"Digitalis is the name of the medicine, Wil. It's used to help people with heart trouble, and it comes right from the foxglove flower. I'm also going to give you some nitroglycerine."

Well, that almost did it for Wil. Now he figured for sure that the boy had wasted his money in medical school.

"Now you're going to blow me up, and I'll already have the flowers in my hand. How convenient!" he said laughing.

"The nitroglycerine is a small pill that you carry with you all the time. If you start to feel a pain in your chest or shortness of breath, you put one under your tongue, and in just a few seconds, you'll feel better. The other one is to be taken every day in the morning, and if you follow my directions, you'll live to be an old man yet."

Wil laughed, "I think I'm already there boy, and I'm starting to feel older all the time. Thanks, Matt. You're a good man."

Wil and Matt walked outdoors into the snow and went over to the general store. Wil was the first through the door and was greeted with a warm hello by the owner. He was looking for some licorice and hard candy for Ma. She needed cheering up, and Wil figured this would do it for sure. They brought their treasure home, and like Wil figured, Ma appreciated it.

"How was your checkup? Are you alright? Tell me!"

She was all over Wil and was not going to take candy for an answer. She kept at the poor man until he asked Matt to give her the report. She, at first, was a bit nervous about it, but when he finished the report, she felt much better. Like Matt said, he'd live to be an old man yet, if he did what the doctor told him.

Chapter 25: A Hard Winter

The winter snowstorms were starting to come a little more frequently now, and each one piled up on the previous to make for some early shoveling. It seemed that each night it added more to the pile. After each hard snow, Wil hitched up Jack and Topsy and plowed snow down to the main road. This was no small job since it took some time to get the two horses harnessed. He hitched them to the steel plow blade and drove them from behind. The horses liked to have work to do, since they spent most of their time during winters in the barn.

Wil had to admit that this constant shoveling was getting the best of him, but the chores still got done, and the hogs were taken care of. Ma kept the fire going in the cook stove, and at night there was a fire in the hearth to take the chill off the rest of the house. Matt's room was empty now, and they had hung a heavy blanket over the doorway so that they didn't have to heat it. They had put up a lot of hardwood this year, but you never knew what kind of winter you'd get especially here on the river. The old saying about having half your wood and half your hay on New Years Day never quite held true around here. That was more for the warmer country around southern Minnesota. Up here when you got to the first of February, you were about halfway to spring and green grass. The winters here were tough, but so were the residents.

Wil had gotten up a bit earlier than usual this morning and was looking outside at the river when Ma came out.

"I heard the river booming this morning. It must be making ice pretty hard. Looks like it's at least twenty-five below."

"When I went outside last night, the northern lights were really dancing too," said Ma. "This winter has been quite a bit worse than in a while. Good thing we put up a lot of feed for the animals."

Wil sat in his chair by the fire and looked at his wife of these many years. He thought back on the times when they had to get the boy dressed warmly for his walk to the schoolhouse. It wasn't that far, but even a couple miles can be tough for a kid when the snow's deep. On one afternoon, Wil decided to walk to the general store to see if there was any mail. As he walked in the boys tracks, he noticed that three wolves had followed him. Panic gripped him, and he hurried his step. Before long, he was running, hoping all the time that he wouldn't see anything laying in the path. He looked up, and there was the school house ahead. The three wolves left the boys tracks a couple hundred yards from the school. Wil rushed inside and surprised the whole class by his instant appearance. He saw the boy standing at the blackboard, and his heart beat hard with joy.

These were tough times for all the critters, so Wil started walking the path with his son twice a day. All of the people in the area were seeing wolves and decided to try to trap them. Several men in the community were good trappers, and they gathered at the general store to make a plan. There were a total of fifty good Victor jump traps between the men, and they had a lot of muskrats to use as bait. They divided the area up into blocks, and each checked his sets daily. During the first week, they had taken five big timber wolves, several coyotes, and five foxes. The next weeks take was a lot smaller, and they figured that they had gotten most of them. Hard winters made for tough times for man and animals alike.

"It's about time to think about the Christmas tree, Wil," said Ma. "You got one picked out yet?"

"What day is it?" He looked at the calendar. "My gosh, woman, how the time has gone by this winter. It's only a week until Christmas! I'll put on the snowshoes today and take a look around on the other side of the river. There is a small spot that burned a few years back, and there's a lot of nice trees coming back."

"We need a special one this year, Wil. We got us a new woman in the family."

They both smiled at the thought of a holiday with the family next door. Wil especially remembered his surprise last year when Matt gave them the rocking chairs. He was a good man and had filled an empty place in their hearts.

As they sat at the table eating breakfast, they heard those familiar footsteps crunching in the snow. In walked Matt and Jane, snow falling from their coats and hats.

"Come in. Come in," Ma said.

"It's a cold one today," said Jane. "I threw a snowball at Matt, and most of it went down the inside of his shirt."

Matt was standing near the cookstove trying to dry his snow soaked shirt.

She laughed, and Matt made a fist at her.

Ma went to the cookstove and put the coffee on the table for their guests.

"Thanks, Ma."

After a half an hour talking about Christmas gifts and cookies, the conversation turned a bit more serious. Matt looked at Jane and winked at her. He put on his most serious face and turned to Ma.

"Ma, we got something pretty important to tell you folks. We been trying to hold off, but we can't much longer."

Ma got a serious look on her face and turned to Wil, putting her hand on his arm. She was worried and knew that it was something bad.

"We're going to have a baby," said Jane.

It took a few seconds for the good news to register, and then their little cabin exploded in laughter and excited voices. This was about the best news that they had ever gotten. A baby, a grandchild. There were tears of joy in the old couples face. Wil always had a small nervous twitch in the corner of his mouth, and it showed a bit more right now. Matt held Ma's hand and smiled along with her. He was going to be a father, and he thought of all the things that he and Wil would do with the new hunter. If it was a girl, it would be the same. She would hunt with them and learn all there was about the outdoors. Thoughts of the new baby flooded their heads, and each in their own way had plans for the yet unborn child. Ma thought of teaching the youngster to sew, and Wil thought about fishing. This was going to be a Christmas like they hadn't had in quite a while.

"Have you told your folks yet?" asked Ma.

"No," said Jane. "We're going over there this afternoon for dinner. I wonder how my mother will take it. She always wanted a granddaughter."

"She'll be as happy as we are," said Ma.

"Dad will be thinking about a helper at the lumber yard," said Jane. "He wants a grandson for sure."

Wil said, "We'll be happy with whatever it is. This family has been blessed again, Matt. I guess these old eyes have seen a lot, but having a new grandchild will surely be about the best."

The group smiled and drank their coffee. There were so many words to say that they seemed to run together with nobody listening and everyone talking. Visions of a child opening Christmas presents ran through the old man's thoughts. He could almost see the new baby's smile. Life had once again taken a turn for the better.

Christmas Eve was a wonderful event for the family. Matt and Jane came over to Wil's cabin early to help with the chores. All the while the men folk were out in the barn, the women busied themselves cooking and baking. Ma had canned several quarts of mince meat, and there were pies to bake. Jane brought over some canned apples and made a beautiful apple pie. There were many kinds of cookies and candies, all colored with sprinkles and decorations. Jane's folks were coming as well and arrived at around 6:00 p.m. for dinner. The whole house took on a cheery glow, and soon the sounds of sleigh bells coming into the yard broke the silence. Mr. and Mrs. Robinson had arrived at the cabin in a horse drawn cutter. The weather was extremely cold, but the thought of the evening warmed their hearts. They came into the cabin and were greeted warmly by Wil and Ma. Matt took their coats and lap robes and handed them a holiday drink of mulled cider. The hot cinnamon and apple flavors tasted good after a ride in the cold and snowy night air.

Dinner was a feast of sausages and other smoked meats. There was pickled herring from the store and smoked salmon on crackers. Ma had made some kind of rice pudding that smelled sweetly of nutmeg. Jane brought some of her favorites too, like lefse and lutefisk. These were Scandinavian dishes and not enjoyed widely among folks of other cultures. There was always a lot of joking about the lutefisk. It was a quivering gelatinous mass of codfish served with a cream sauce, and the lefse was like a thin potato pancake spread with butter and topped with strawberry preserves. It was rolled up and eaten with delight.

All of them ate heartily and enjoyed each other's company. Conversation turned to all of the gifts under the tree, and Wil passed them out one by one with a big smile. The radio played Christmas carols, and they all became quiet when the President wished the nation a very merry Christmas during his fireside chat. Everyone opened their gifts and thanked the givers graciously. There were sweaters, mittens, aprons, and candles for gifts, along with many other gifts of food. They sang some of their old favorites like Jingle Bells and a new one called White Christmas. The house sparkled from the many oil lamps and candles, and soon it was time to go home. The coats were brought out, and Jane and Mrs. Robinson hugged Ma and thanked her for such a wonderful evening. Mr. and Mr. Robinson said, "Merry Christmas," and went out to turn the team of horses around in the yard. Matt and Jane jumped in back and covered themselves with a robe. The others got in and headed the team toward Matt and Jane's house, bells jingling in the cold snowy air. Then, it was off down the road to the Robinson's with the team throwing up huge clouds of snow behind them.

Sunday morning found the whole family sitting in church with all of their neighbors. The Lutheran preacher led the choir in "Oh Little Town of Bethlehem" and several old songs familiar to the congregation. This was a very special day, for Wil and he prayed that he and Ma be given the years to watch the new child grow.

March came and with it some warmer weather and a hint of spring. The days got warm and turned the roads to mud, and in the evening, it went back down below zero. The ups and downs during this time of year were hard on the snowbound families. Everyone wanted to see the snow go and stay gone, but it was some weeks, yet, until it was time to think of things like gardens. In the old barn, sheep were lambing, and the cattle presented Wil with a new pair of calves. The pasture out back was still covered with two feet of snow, but every day it let go a bit more of it's strangle hold on the land. Chickadees were singing their phee-bee song, and that meant that spring was near. The river had a coating of water flowing on top of the ice on the warmer days, and in the evening, it was back to solid again with temperatures below zero. The roof on Wil's cabin needed repair, and when the sun got the water running, the roof leaked like a sieve. It did so every year, and it seemed that there was no use trying to find the leak.

Matt's practice grew, and he was seeing at least four patients every day. Jane was his constant companion and a caring nurse. Her days sometimes got a bit too long, and Matt made her take a day off to rest up. He was keeping a close eye on her condition. She was a strong woman, but he didn't want anything to happen to her or the baby.

Wil was out in the barn taking a mental inventory of his hay and grain when he started to feel weak, like he had worked too hard. He sat down on the milking stool and waited for it to pass. The feeling seemed to get worse, like it wasn't going to give up without a fight. He thought for a moment about the pills that Matt had given him for such times. He took the small bottle out of his pants pocket and opened it carefully. By now the sweat was running down his face even though it was still cold in the barn. He took one of the small pills and placed it under his tongue like Matt had said. He waited for a few minutes and noticed that it wasn't helping at all, and he was getting weaker. He took another and waited. This time, he got relief from the chest pain. He sat quietly in the barn trying to get the strength to get up and go to the cabin. Once inside, he told Ma that he was a bit tired and was going to take a nap. She smiled, and Wil disappeared into the bedroom. He laid down on the bed and pulled the feather tick over himself. He was still shivering when he fell asleep.

When he awoke it was morning. He had been pretty tired, but he didn't think he was that much in need of sleep. Ma had pulled his night cap over his head and let him sleep in his clothes. He went out into the kitchen and sat at the table.

"Good morning, Wil. Do you want some coffee?"

"Sure. I was pretty tired last night."

"You mean yesterday afternoon, don't you?"

"Guess so. What's for breakfast?"

"Suppose about anything you want," she said with a grin. "How about some toast and jelly?"

Wil went out to do the chores and found that Ma had beaten him to most of them. All that she didn't do was the hogs, and that was because of a mean boar that he kept for breeding. He was back in the house within an hour and had some more coffee. His wife did her best to take care of her man, but sometimes he wouldn't cooperate with her. He had work to do, and Ma wanted him to rest today. He started back out the door, and Ma grabbed his coat and hung it back on the nail.

"Today, I need a man's help here in the house," she said, and she wasn't smiling. Wil knew that look, and she meant what she said.

Chapter 26: Ice Fishing

Winter was wearing hard on everyone, and it was getting a bit more difficult to stay cheerful. In spite of the long nights, several neighbors still got together on the weekends for card games and conversation. It helped, but there was still little to do to make spring come any sooner. It passed one day at a time, one slow day at a time.

Wil's day started early at around 5:00 a.m. He opened the door to let in some fresh air and then built a good fire to take the chill off the little cabin. It was time to build a pot of good coffee. He ground fresh coffee beans and used the coldest water he could find, and that meant a trip to the well. When the coffee started smelling pretty good, Ma emerged from the bedroom with a big smile on her face. A quick kiss on Wil's weathered old face was always the way to start a good day. After he had poured them a cup of coffee, he turned on the Zenith battery radio. Stations from as far away as Duluth usually came in quite well, but at times the best reception came from way up in Winnipeg, Canada. The radio needed to be replaced, but without electricity, the old battery type had to do.

After the last of the coffee was gone, it was time for Wil to get the chores done. There were two cows to be milked, hogs to be fed, and the team of horses to be taken care of. On this negative thirty-five degree day, all of the animals got an extra bit of hay or oats. The sheep were starting to show the results of last years breeding. He headed to the chicken coop and picked up nearly a dozen eggs.

As Wil came back into the cabin, he noticed that some of the smile had worn off Ma's face. He thought for a moment and asked if she would like to go to town with him and maybe get a piece of pie and coffee. That perked her right up, and in no time, she was making plans for the trip. She needed some groceries, and Wil needed a sack of oats and one of cracked corn. Then, they would go to the café for pie before they went home.

Wil headed back outside into the extreme cold and hitched up the team to the cutter. Even the horses were glad to have something to pull. By the time that he finished harnessing the team, Ma was ready with a couple blankets. She jumped in and snuggled up right beside Wil. She threw the blankets over his legs, and with a quick whistle, they were off down the road with the wind blowing hard in their faces. As they neared the road, Wil slowed the team to a canter and turned to the left going away from the store. Wil slapped the team with the reins, and away they went at a full gallop. The team loved to be worked, and you could see it by the way they pulled. Wil saw a wider place in the road and turned the team around heading back toward the general store at a slow trot. It seemed that even the livestock needed a bit of time outside.

As they neared the store, Wil slowed the team and tied them up to the post near the steps. When they entered the store, Milo was right there to welcome them.

"Good to see you folks. It seems like I see more neighbors in this cold than I do when it's warm. We had about forty below today."

"I don't think we had that cold, but just the same, it's a chilly one," said Wil. "Ma does need some supplies though, so I'll sit here by the wood stove and warm up some."

"Good idea, Wil. What do you think about going fishing tomorrow? Them Peterson boys caught quite a few nice lake trout yesterday."

Now that sounded like a pretty good plan to Wil. He sure did like ice fishing.

"You bet I'll go, and I know of a few more men that'll go with us. I'm heading for the café before we head home, and I'm betting there's a few there that will go, too."

They agreed to meet at the store at 10:00 a.m. and bring all their gear with them. Milo had some big minnows, and that worked pretty well for lake trout. It seemed that the plan was set.

Wil and Ma headed back to the cutter and on down to the feed store. Inside, they found a couple more fisherman warming up by the big wood stove. Wil picked up an additional four there. Then, it was off for pie and coffee. There was nearly a full house in the café, and several men wanted to go along. It looked like they needed three teams and cutters. There were fourteen so far, and by morning, there would be more. The only way to get through winters that were this cold was to face them head on and go about your business.

The next morning Wil hitched up the team and headed to the general store. It was another cold morning with the temperature once again close to forty below. As Wil got out of the cutter, he could hear the ice booming on the river. When he walked inside the store, there was quite a crowd that greeted him. It looked like nearly twenty men, some young and some up in years, but they all had one thing in common, they loved to fish.

The men and equipment were loaded into the cutters, and they headed out of town toward the south, and Big Jessie Lake. It was about six miles away, but with a team and cutter, the trip went quickly. The tracks of the Peterson boys were still there, and it looked like they had driven right out onto the lake. There was still a lot of ice, so it held nearly anything. As the men started to chisel holes in the ice, they found a grand total of thirty inches of ice. This cold weather made ice at a fierce rate.

Within a half hour, all the holes were open, and the lines were set. Fishing started a bit slow, but within an hour, Wil pulled up a nice five pounder. That got everyone pretty excited. The fish were flopping on the ice pretty soon, but there weren't any big ones. Old Arne decided to go on down the lake a bit and try it there. He walked off a quarter mile or so and chopped another hole. Everyone was watching him and saw that he was catching some. The fishing was picking up, and everyone had some big ones, some nearing ten pounds. This had turned out to be a pretty good idea after all.

As the sun started to get closer to the trees and the color of the snow slowly turned a slate gray, some of the men decided to head home for the day and warm up. The temperature was again starting to drop. The team headed to shore, and soon the rest of the bunch also decided to call it a day. They pulled up their lines and got everything back into the cutter. Wil looked over at old Arne and gave him a whistle.

Wil and the rest got in and drove the team over to Arne. They made a big circle around him and stopped the cutter nearby. One of the men got out and walked toward Arne crouched down with the wind at his back. He didn't move, and it became evident that old Arne was dead. All the men gathered around him not saying a thing. Wil touched Arne on the shoulder, and it seemed like he had been dead a while because his shoulder was stiff. On the ice lay a total of four big lake trout with one going way over thirty pounds. He was quite a fisherman, even in the last moments of his life.

Arne had been a good friend to a lot of the men and had known them all for many years. In general, they all had a hard time feeling the appropriate sorrow. He had no wife or children and no other relatives. The whole town had always looked on him as one of their own, and now he was gone. His whole life had been one of doing what he loved most, no matter what it was.

They loaded his body into the cutter and brought him back to town. Not much was said on the return trip. When they got back to the general store, the men all went inside, and Milo brought out a bottle of his finest brandy, and the men all gave a toast to a friend. No tears were shed, but in the course of the evening, several bottles were emptied, and many stories were told of a great man and good friend. It had been quite a fishing trip.

Chapter 27: Summer

Winter gradually eased its grip on the small community. Kids were playing in the mud puddles, making small dams and sailing paper boats down their miniature rivers. Nearby, the mighty Bigfork River was rushing northward to the sea. Sometimes it was so loud that the residents had to move inside to carry on a conversation. The boulders in the rapids sent the water flying thirty feet into the air.

As the spring runoff subsided, the men took their favorite places below the rapids and fished for walleyes. These weren't large fish, but they had a good flavor and could be cleaned to remove the bones for the small kids. Spearing for northern pike was all done, and there were some large ones taken that year, with some over forty pounds. The men waded the small creeks and pushed the fish to the others standing upstream. They speared them and hauled them out onto the bank. The cold water of the winter made them taste very mild. Wil brought one home for Ma to cook, and she did her usual fantastic job. She soaked the fish in water and vinegar for some time and rinsed it clear of any sour taste. Then she stuffed it with bread stuffing. After a couple hours baking in the oven of the cookstove, the fish came out perfectly browned, and even the bones were soft like canned salmon bones.

Jane was starting to show a bit more, and Ma delighted in knitting things for the grand baby. She brought them to Jane's house, and they talked about whether it was a boy or girl. Of course, the men wanted a boy, and the women wanted a girl, but in general, they all wanted a healthy baby. Matt was spending some of his free time in Wil's old shed building a cradle for the baby. It, too, was made out of beautiful pieces of diamond willow, Matt's favorite wood. The project was a labor of love, and he took time with each piece, working the wood to perfection.

Life on the river was getting back to what people called normal. The snow had long since disappeared, and the general store was doing a brisk business in garden supplies. Seeds of all varieties were for sale in a brightly colored display. The Post Office delivered several boxes of chicks to different farms in the area, so that meant that spring had indeed arrived in the Bigfork Valley. The mailman had even delivered the usual boxes of bees. This meant a trying time for him, since a few bees always hitchhiked on the outside of the box.

The mailman was in the general store talking to a couple customers about the mail business. He told how he had used a horse and small buggy for as long as there had been R.F.D., and as time went by, he finally got the money saved to purchase a car. This made his life a lot better, and the mail was delivered in style winter and summer.

He told about one day when he tried to pull up to a dairy farmer's mailbox. He saw that the whole herd of cows had gotten out of the pasture and were standing around the mailbox. First, he waited to see if they would move, and they just stood there. Then, he decided that he would try to push his way through gently with the car. That didn't seem to work either. There were cows everywhere, so he figured that he'd honk the horn.

Dairy cows, being a rather nervous lot, and the fact that they were on new green grass, made for a most serious situation. As the melodious sounds leaped from the shiny chrome horn, the cattle all jumped at once, and being of just the right height and position, dropped copious amounts of smelly manure right through his car window, all over the mail and him, too.

He had learned a valuable lesson that day and next time would do things differently. The remainder of the customers on his route that day were somewhat perplexed by the condition of the mail.

The mailman's day saw the usual complaints about stamp prices, and sometimes there was a gift from a customer. Most times it was a piece of cake or maybe the dreaded cookie. Early in his career, he carelessly bit down on a fresh baked cookie only to discover that it was crisscrossed inside with dog hairs. That cured him from ever eating route gifts unless he personally knew the giver.

The next day Wil harnessed the team to the plow and made a nice garden spot. Then, he ran the manure spreader over it to give the ground some fuel to grow the garden. He ran a disc over that and then a harrow. The ground was ready for Wil and warm weather to get started growing. He decided to use a lot of space on potatoes this year because of Matt and Jane. He and Ma always planted a lot of peas. These garden treasures were always sown when the ground was still too cold for other crops and were a bit intense to work with. The thoughts of fresh green peas and new potatoes in cream sauce made all the hard work worthwhile.

It was the first of June, and the ground had warmed sufficiently to take seed. Planting took a great deal of time, and each kind of seed had to be planted at a different depth. He planted many hills of cucumbers, so he also had to plant a row of dill as well. There was leaf lettuce to be used in wilted lettuce salad. Ma tore the lettuce up in bite size pieces and fried some bacon. She poured some sweetened vinegar over the lettuce and added the bacon, grease and all. This was another of those spring delights that Matt had never tasted before. He raved about it for days.

It took Wil a full day to plant the potatoes. There were twelve long rows, and they needed constant care throughout the summer. It seemed that the potato bugs were always trying to get ahead of him. He hilled the potatoes, and that was a backbreaking job as well. Over on the end of the garden closest to the house, he planted his tomatoes. These had to be cared for all the time. He staked them up so that they didn't fall over. Then, there was the last section where he planted all of the things that he loved most. There were Brussels sprouts, cabbage, carrots, beets, onions, and radishes. When all the seed was in the ground, they got a nice long rain to get the seed going. The roof leaked some more, but this was the time of year for such things.

Wil's health was a constant problem for him, and Matt did his best to keep up with it, using the newest medicines. He was getting a little long of tooth as the old men used to say. He never discussed his age, and nobody asked. When he got tired, he rested, and when he felt good, he worked. That was good enough for him. He and Ma had a good life on the river, and it looked like it would continue for a good while yet.

There had been many changes throughout his life, but one thing that remained the same was that he always had his wife there to share the bad times with. He didn't think of it in so many words, but she was the left hand that washed the right. All that he did in some way related to her. She was his helpmate.

When the hot part of summer arrived, it was time to put up hay for the animals. This was an intense job and required the help of at least one other man. Wil used the team to pull the mower, and he turned the hay over the next day to make sure that it dried right. If there was a wet spot, it could catch the barn on fire. He used the drop rake to pull it into piles, all the while praying that it wouldn't rain and ruin the crop. Matt helped, and the hay was in the barn in three days. There was a little hay left in the field, and Wil asked Matt to go along with him in the hay wagon and get it. Matt took a pitchfork and proceeded to load the wagon.

"Dammit, boy! What are you doing?"

Matt watched as the old man reached into the stack of hay and lifted it into the wagon. He gave it a try and got a small handful. Wil could lift a huge stack with one hand.

"How'd you do that?"

"Watch."

He reached into the top of a large stack, and with a few turns of his wrist, lifted a huge pile again. Matt gave it his best try and came up way short again. Wil, once more, showed him how to do it.

"You reach inside as far as you can and grab a handful. Then, you turn it and get a better grip. You turn it some more and get a new grip and when you lift, you get all that is above your wrist but you have to do that with both arms or you tip over." He grinned at Matt.

Matt tried again, and this time he had it figured out. He had such a stack that he couldn't lift it. He fell on the stack laughing.

"You know, Matt, the whole idea when you farm alone is that you have to do the most work you can with as little time spent on it as possible. You learn to work smarter so that you can move on to the next job."

Evening came, and they had all the hay in the barn. Both of them were a bit tired and dirty, so they decided to take a swim to cool off. Matt looked around to see if anyone was watching and took off his clothes. He ran down the hill toward the river like he had done so many times and jumped as far as he could. He came up spluttering and grinning. The water was cool and felt good on his parched skin. Wil was a bit more subdued and waded in with his bar of lye soap. They cleaned up from head to toe, and Wil waded back out of the river. He was dressed again in no time and walked toward the house. As he walked by Matt's pile of clothes, he grinned with a little mischievous smile and picked them up to take them along into the house.

A short while later, Matt walked up the bank to where he had left his clothes and couldn't find them. He was in a bit of a predicament. He didn't want to go inside naked, and there was absolutely nothing there to cover himself with, not even a fig leaf. He studied the problem for a second and ran back down the hill again and dove back into the water. He swam downstream until he got to his cabin and waded out and walked inside. Jane, of course, had seen him naked before, so he opened the cabin door and just walked on in.

There, sitting at the kitchen table, were the women of the Ladies Aid Society from the church. It was too late to retreat, so Jane threw him a towel to cover with, and he walked calmly into the bedroom. It was hard for him, but he stayed in there until all the laughter had subsided and the ladies had left. His professional reputation was intact, but not by much. Ma was there, too, so he really could have went inside with Wil to get his clothes. He thought that next time, he might do things a bit differently, but he wasn't exactly sure how.

July came around and with it the big Fourth of July celebration. There were contests of all forms. Wil's favorite was the pie eating contest put on by the church. It cost him a dollar to enter, and he figured that he got more than his moneys worth in pie. He tied for last place, but he did that every year.

You could enter running races, three legged races, wheelbarrow races, and in fact, there were races for almost anything you could name. Baking contests drew many entrants from the community. Prizes were small, but the recognition of a win was what mattered. For the young kids, they threw a few dollars worth of coins in a pile of sawdust. The scramble for coins drew a lot of attention. Late afternoon brought the band and a dance for everyone. The ladies wore numbers, and the men had to buy a dance ticket for a nickel if they wanted to dance with someone special. All the money went to the orphans fund. Matt waited his turn in line and bought a ticket to dance with Jane. He looked to find her and found that she already had a partner. He waited patiently, and then another gentleman danced with her, and another. He was getting a bit discouraged when she finally walked over to him and asked if he had bought a ticket. He stood up and took her around the floor several turns, enjoying the music and the rare beauty of his wife. She was getting bigger, and her tummy came between them a bit. Matt laughed and gave her a kiss on the cheek.

Evening came, and with it, the fireworks. The kids had sparklers and lady finger firecrackers to shoot off. The show over the river was quite spectacular with lots of oohs and awws. Then, the dance continued until late for the adults. When midnight came, there was a meal served by the ladies, and everyone donated appropriately to their cause. After that, there were many goodbyes, and the entire community went home, except for a few wayward lumberjacks. Dirty Annie's saloon was still doing a brisk business into the small hours of the morning.

Summer passed, and the gardens grew. Wil and Ma picked several different kinds of berries, and she canned them for winter. The color of those quarts lined up on the counter was splendid and marked the beginning of harvest. As things ripened, they were canned or preserved in some manner for winter use. Life on the river was the same every year, but harvest brought a certain excitement. It was, again, like getting paid for all of your labor.

Jane was getting closer to delivering a new baby, and the excitement grew in the family. Each morning, Ma appeared to see how Jane was doing and see whether or not she felt anything that resembled labor pains. It was almost getting to be a joke. As soon as Ma opened the door, Jane looked at her and shook her head no and laughed. They had become close friends, and she appreciated the older woman's advice on all sorts of subjects, but Ma was always careful not to give her opinion unless asked.

Matt had finished the cradle and brought it into the house for Jane to decorate with lace. It had turned out nice, and she was impatient to see the new occupant. In time, they would have to add another room onto the house, but for now it was the right size for them.

August came, and with it, the dog days of summer. The heat was making the gardens grow nicely, and the evening rains kept the soil from drying. Each day, Wil walked the rows of potatoes with a small can of kerosene. He'd pick the potato bugs and drop them into the can. It was a constant battle to keep ahead of the insects, but he was determined not to let them win.

"Wil! Come quick!" yelled Ma.

He came on the run, wondering what had happened. Ma was standing there with a grin on her face.

"Jane's in labor. I'm going back over there to help, and I want you to go and tell Matt."

Wil got into the car and drove to Matt's office. When he walked in, Matt was finishing up with some paperwork. He looked up and saw the look on Wil's face and knew it was important.

"Jane's in labor. Ma's with her now. She's delivered a lot of babies and says that there's no hurry."

Matt dropped everything and got in his car. He drove slowly behind Wil, but he sure wanted to go faster. This was a big day for them all, but especially Matt and Jane. This was the start of their family.

Matt walked into the cabin and saw his wife standing at the stove cooking lunch.

"What are you doing? You should be lying down."

"Now, Matt, I'm not even close to having this baby yet. It could be several hours away."

Matt, with all his years of studying medicine had, just had it all thrown out the window, and realized he wasn't in charge here. This was a woman thing, and he was to sit there and help when called upon. He could help other people, but this was a family thing, and Ma had the situation under control.

The hours went by slowly, and Matt sat with his wife through some hard contractions. He felt helpless and held Jane's hand for support. He took her pulse without her knowing it, keeping a mental note of everything. Her contractions were timed with Matt's pocket watch, and the labor was progressing nicely. By supper time, she was having labor pains every three minutes and had to be getting close. She walked around the house for a while and then went back to bed. Her water broke, and that speeded the labor up quite a bit. By 7:00 p.m. she was having hard labor, and Ma came in to check her. Jane was sweating, and Matt was holding a wet cloth to her head. Ma told him it was time for him to go out in the other room, but he flatly refused. His place was with his wife, and he was right there if he were needed.

Jane was pushing hard now, and the baby was getting closer to joining the family. With one great push, young Wil came into the world. He had black hair, and his dad's nose. Ma had him cleaned up and sitting on Jane's chest in no time. Jane looked over at her husband and saw the tears streaming down his cheeks.

Chapter 28: Young Wil

Life in Matt and Jane's house took on a significantly different pace. There was a new voice in the cabin, and that small voice determined when and for how long each of them was allowed to sleep. He had a strong voice and in a short time they got to know what each kind of a cry meant. There was the one where he was in a panic to be fed. There was one where he needed a fresh diaper, and there was even one where he needed to be held and talked to. They got to know their son, and their lives were made better with his presence. He smiled at an early age and that gave Matt much pleasure. He held the boy and talked to him in great detail of all the things he would see and do. He talked of great hunting trips and fishing in the spring. He held toys up for him to see and read him stories. Matt wanted the boy to know everything.

As the child grew older and got to the age where he could sit up, Matt noticed that he would rather lay down than sit. He didn't cry very much, but he smiled and cooed to get attention. He said Mama and Dadda, and that got big grins from both parents alike. Wil and Ma doted on the boy and gave him as much attention as they could. They never came to Matt and Jane's house without bringing something for young Wil.

When Wil was two years old, Matt noticed that he wasn't doing the things that other patients of his did at the same age. He had a fear that something was wrong with his son and didn't want to say anything that might scare Jane. Wil could sit for a long time staring out the window, never making a sound. At the dinner table one evening, Matt felt that he had to say something to Jane. As soon as he broached the subject, Jane started to cry. Things that had been held inside for months came out like a great flood. She, too, had been worried and didn't want to concern Matt. He had come to the conclusion several weeks ago that their son was mentally retarded.

Jane had blamed herself and didn't want to talk about it. Matt had felt plenty of blame on his shoulders, too, and thought it was his fault, but in reality, it was no ones fault. Between the parents, there were times that felt so sorrowful that it was like a death in the family. There was dread of his outcome and who would take care of him after they were gone. Sometimes God makes a special child, and their house had been blessed with one. He needed a lot of love and care, but he could still have a good life.

The seasons on the river came and went, and the boy grew to be his grandpa's constant shadow. Little Wil referred to his grandpa as Poppa and his grandma as Nana. They did farm work together, and when Matt was done at the office, he took over. Little Wil grew into a good looking boy of five and was nearly ready to start school. There were some tough decisions that had to be made. Would he go to school with the rest of the kids or stay home and have Mom and Dad teach him all that he could learn? The decision was made one evening when Matt and Jane invited the teacher to dinner. They had a nice meal, and the conversation turned to little Wil. They all sat at the dinner table talking about what they thought he could learn and if he might disrupt the other students. The decision was made to send him to school. He had to work very hard, but little Wil wanted to give it a try. He had already developed a good vocabulary and wanted to learn. Some things were nearly impossible for him, but others he could master. Only time would tell what he could and couldn't do.

In class he sat still and didn't offer much, but on the playground he was active and seemed to have friends his age. It was in the classroom that he had the trouble. He could recite his ABC's and could read numbers. He was read to each evening and helped with the things that he couldn't do. Reading was very hard for him, and math concepts were out of the question.

There were a couple older boys that made fun of him, and that made him sad. He knew that he was different, but he didn't know how. The teacher was careful not to ask him things that he couldn't do in front of the class. At times, she asked him a question about geography or science, and as long as he didn't have to write anything, he did well. He never could exactly come up with the idea about some things, but he had a good memory. School was tough for him, but it only lasted for six hours a day, and he could handle that. Then, it was home to change clothes and get back into the world that he was most comfortable with. He had a quick cookie and some milk and headed to Poppa's house on a dead run. Wil always expected the boy about the same time each day, and it filled his heart with joy to hear the child yell from outside. It kept the old man young to have the child near him. There were so many things that he needed to be taught, and Wil felt that there was so little time. His health had been going down hill for some time, and even the gardening was starting to be too much for him.

Matt told Wil that there was a problem with his lungs, but he didn't say what it was. The old man was getting to the point where breathing sometimes was a chore, and he had to slow down. The boy sensed that Wil was having trouble and sometimes would go stand by him, with his hand in Poppa's pocket. There was a closeness that Wil had never felt before, and he loved the boy deeply, just the way he was. God had given him a grandson in his last years as a gift to be cherished. The child had a heart full of love for everyone and gave it generously.

The summer of little Wil's seventh year was special for the whole family. He had learned to do many things around the house, and he helped by sweeping his dad's office on Saturdays to earn his allowance. He had learned to pick potato bugs with Poppa and to hoe the corn. He could pick raspberries for dinner, but he would rather pop them right into his mouth.

Summer turned cooler, and the nights got longer. Harvest was under way, and work lasted from daylight to dark. These were hard days for the old man. His years were catching up to him, and lately he had been losing weight. Ma helped where she could, but sometimes they had to rely on Matt for his strength. The crops were nearly put up for the winter, but this year, Wil had to hire a man to put up his wood for him. The physical exertion left him winded, and every once in a while, he went behind the shed where no one could see him and opened the little bottle of nitroglycerine. He was getting weaker each day, and the rigors of life were showing on his face.

"Are you interested in going to Colorado this year?" Matt asked.

"Don't think that I could handle a trip up that high. Even when I was a young man, the altitude used to get me for the first couple days. Sure would like to take little Wil there, though."

"I've got an idea. What do you think about going to Montana for mule deer? The altitude isn't nearly as bad, and the hunting's pretty good, too."

Wil thought for a moment, and with a renewed sparkle in his eye said, "Lets do it."

The trip was planned for the first week in October, and little Wil grew more excited by the day. He was now seven years old and a pretty fair shot with his .223 rifle. The men packed the car with all it would hold, and then the trailer was loaded with the tent and the food locker. Ma sent a lot of canned stuff and enough cookies to last until spring. Jane had made rolls and bread for them, so all that was left was to pack it all away.

Matt included a supply of medicine that he might need for Wil and told no one about it. He took a lot of extra clothes for the boy and declared the job done. The rifles had been cleaned several times, and little Wil was adept at taking his apart and putting it back together again. He was raised around guns and knew how to handle them even at an early age.

The family waved it's goodbyes and headed down the road at first light. The trip required three days if all went well. The boy got to see a whole new part of the world. He asked a lot of questions, and Wil was always glad to take the time to answer. Each night on the way there, they set up a small camp and slept on the prairie. The stars were as bright as at home, but the music of the prairie was different. They heard the songs of the hawks as they migrated south and the prairie falcons as they searched for mice. Night time brought the campfires and stories from the two friends as they recalled times past when they were on the Roseau together. Young Wil listened carefully.

Chapter 29: The Grizzly

One evening as they sat watching the fire, Wil started to tell Matt and young Wil of a time when he was much younger, a time when he hunted the elk of Wyoming. It was a time when he and his brother Tom had been quite close. They traveled the high country during the fall looking for an opportunity to try something different, and both of them loved to hunt.

"We camped one night along side of a stream with nearby granite peaks reaching toward the sky. It had the feel of a cathedral and was so quiet you could hear a mouse breathe for miles. Wyoming had few roads into the back country, so if you wanted to hunt it, you had to use horses.

We finished our supper, and I was busy cleaning the dishes in the stream. I heard a sound coming from the south, and soon a rider came into their camp. His horse looked like it had been ridden hard, and the man in the saddle didn't look much better.

I told him to step down and sit a spell, and he thanked me. He asked if we had any coffee. I told him that we just cleaned the pot, but we could make another.

Tom headed back to the stream to get another pot of water, and I put a few pieces of wood on the fire.

The man said that he had been out quite a while and hadn't eaten a thing in two days. He asked if we could spare some food. Tom looked at him and saw that this was a man that needed food for sure. He dug into the trunk and pulled out a can of beans and a couple potatoes.

Tom asked if that would be alright, and the man said that it would do just fine. His name was Travis Hart.

We all shook hands, and I told him that we were there to hunt elk, but they were mighty hard to catch up with since we didn't know the country very well. We wanted to try for a grizzly, but neither of us knew much about the area.

With that, the man broke down and cried. He said that he and his son Jimmy had camped way back up in the hills, and a grizzly bear got his boy. Seems like they were asleep one night in their tent and a bear tore right through the canvas and took him. He mauled Travis, grabbing him at the top of his arm near the shoulder. He bled hard for a while, and eventually got it stopped with a rag tied around it. He was some weak from the loss of blood, but he had to go and find his son. He saddled up and started tracking the bear. He searched for three days by horseback and never did catch up with him. All that he found was part of the boy's clothes. He ran out of food and was headed back down the mountain for supplies. He had his son's horse, still saddled, and a pack mule strung behind him.

Tom untied the animals and tethered them near some good grass and water. He pulled off the saddles and pack frames. The animals looked like they hadn't been fed in quite a while.

Wil had the beans and potatoes ready for Travis and had him sit by the fire. He ate noisily and drank two cups of strong coffee. After he finished eating, the conversation again turned to the bear. He had plans to go back and kill that bear, no matter how long it took him.

Travis shared a tent with the men and slept restlessly through the night. When morning arrived, Tom and I had a fire going, and the pot of coffee was about ready.

"Travis said that it was right nice of us to take in a stray. Tom told him to grab a cup of coffee and pull up a stump. We told him that we were going to give him a hand if we could find some horses, and he was pretty grateful.

Travis said that his spread was only a little more than eight miles from there, and he had plenty of stock to choose from. Then, he had to go home and tell his wife what had happened. He gave us a hand drawn map of how to get to his ranch. Then, he rode off.

We sat for a while talking about the bear. Neither of us had hunted the big ones before, so we didn't know quite what to expect. We had only a week until we had to head back to northern Minnesota. There were chores back home that we had to take care of.

In a short time, we had the camp tore down. We loaded the tent and blankets in the trailer and headed down the road toward the ranch. Tom gave directions, and in fifteen minutes, we pulled into the yard at about the same time Travis did. He tied his animals to the hitching post and walked into the house. A muffled cry came from the house, and I figured that the bad news had been given. A neighbor lady was there with his wife, and she said that she would stay until he came back home.

Travis took the animals back behind the barn into the corral and fed and watered them. He poured a bucket of oats in the feeder and took fresh animals out to be saddled. We decided what to take with us, and it was sparse rations for us all. Tom and I used the same kind of a gun, a 45-70 government that was more than enough for any bear. There were a couple blankets and a canteen of water each with enough shells to do the job.

Some bears covered a lot of territory in a day, and others stayed where they fed the best. I figured that the bear was still in the area.

We mounted up and headed back up the canyon to where they had the run in with the bear. It was a long hard trip for one day, and when we camped for the night, we used the same fire pit that Travis had used, the same camp where the boy had been taken. I looked around the camp site and didn't see anything that looked like bear tracks.

Tom built a good fire, and we sat watching the flames, trying hard to make a plan that made sense. We had no idea where the bear had gone and no tracks to follow. We thought to have each man head in a different direction, but this country was pretty unforgiving to anyone that traveled alone. We all rolled out our blankets near the fire and fell asleep. I was still partly awake when I heard a low growl coming from some heavy brush not far away. Instantly, we were up and reaching for guns. There was no chance at all of seeing anything that time of night that was outside of our campfire light. We sat and looked around for quite some time and again went to sleep.

At daylight, I sat looking into the flames of a morning fire, and Travis was nowhere to be found. In a short time, he came walking back from the heavy brush where he heard the bear last night. He nodded his head and said that now there were fresh tracks to follow. That bear, he thought, wanted the rest of his meal, namely Travis. He had tasted blood when he grabbed his shoulder, and he wanted the rest.

We saddled up and followed Travis through the heavy timber, moving slowly, following the tracks of the grizzly. We seemed to be getting no closer to the bear, and all of the tracks that we saw were at least four hours old.

We stopped for a breather at noon and had a drink of water. I tipped up my canteen and thought that we had better take it easy on the water. We didn't know when he would find more. Tom was still fired up and hurried the rest time some so we could catch up with that bear.

We rode hard for most of the afternoon and by nightfall found a good spot to spend the night by a small stream. All of us were tired out but ready for another day of the same thing tomorrow. We seemed to be getting no closer to the bear.

The next day, Tom picked up the trail again, and we all followed as fast as we could. We crossed one small stream, and it appeared that the bear had jumped across it with one great leap. Travis was a bit concerned because we were following tracks that were leading back to their first camp.

Again, nighttime found us at the same place we had started from the day before. There was something about this animal that I thought of as being almost human. He seemed to have a plan, and we weren't going to ruin it. He was leading us to where he wanted us to be, back at the camp where he had gotten the boy.

After a small meal, we again unrolled our blankets near the fire. Sleep came easily again for all of us, but again during the night Travis heard the bear make one single low growl not too far off. He grabbed his rifle and walked out into the darkness. Tom yelled at him to come back, but Travis wouldn't answer. I kept watching in the direction that he had left, and then a shot rang out in the darkness, and then another, followed by a hard scream. Then, there was silence. I yelled to Travis, but there was no reply. Tom took a turn at yelling.

Still, there was no reply. We sat by the fire with the guns on our laps until the sun started to come up over the hills.

I figured that it wasn't very far, so we went to have a look where the shot came from. We saw a boot and a rifle and little else. There was a lot of blood on the ground. The bear had carried Travis off, moving down the hill into the scrub brush. Tom picked up the blood spattered rifle.

At the time, it seemed to me that the story had played itself out, and that there was no sense in me or Tom getting killed. This bear was a man eater, and I didn't want to lose my brother.

We saddled up and headed down the mountain, Tom holding the reins of a riderless horse. The woman of the house had to be told, and we hoped that there was still someone there with her.

We came to the ranch again near dark. Travis' wife came out, and when she saw the horse without a rider, she knew what had happened. The bear had claimed another of her family. She wept bitter tears and attempted to thank us for trying to help. We drove off down the road and Tom swore never to come back to Wyoming."

Wil sat, staring at the fire, thinking about the tragedy that had befallen Travis and his son, and wondered what had ever become of his wife.

Matt and little Wil sat staring at the old man. The story was finished, and there was no more to be said that night.

The fire was nearly out, and Wil headed for the warmth of his wool blankets.

Chapter 30: The Eye of an Eagle

The third day they arrived at Miles City, Montana and much closer to where they wanted to hunt. They filled up the car with gasoline and got more water for the camp. Little Wil was never more than a step away from Poppa. When they left the little town, they headed north toward the border. An hour's drive and they found a sheltered area with a few trees. The decision was made to camp there, and then the work began again. The first thing was the new tent. It was hard to set up, but it gave them a bit more room than the old one. All of the food was left in the trailer, in case a bear decided to pay them a call. The boy got out all of the cooking gear and set it near the fire. His job was to keep the campsite clean and throw all the small junk into the fire. It gave him a sense of importance and kept him busy.

The camp was all set up by 3:00 p.m., and that gave them some time to go scout the area. This wasn't at all like hunting in Minnesota. From the first look at the countryside, it appeared as flat as one of Wil's pancakes, but as you crossed the land, there were big gullies that contained trees and brush. The does were pretty small, but the bucks had immense racks and hopped like rabbits. It looked like an awkward gait, but they ate up the ground at a fierce rate when they had to.

The boy stood beside Poppa with his hand in the old man's pocket. He didn't say anything, but he pointed at a clump of brush about a hundred yards away. Matt looked at it with his binoculars and saw a huge buck with a rocking chair rack. The sharp eyes of the boy had spotted the critter with no difficulty. None of the group had a gun with them, so they backed out of the area and hoped that the big buck would still be in the same vicinity tomorrow.

The sun had shed its final rays, and the campfire was once again the center of everything. The boy watched the sparks sail upwards slowly into the night sky and asked if God could smell the smoke. Wil said that he was sure He could. In the boy's simple way, he spoke his belief in God and showed the men that the faith of a child was what life was all about.

Morning found the group sitting near the fire, trying to eat some breakfast. The wind had come up, and it had clouded over. The temperature was down to near freezing, and the boy shivered. Wil dropped a coat over his shoulders, and the boy grinned at him. It looked to Matt like it could start snowing at any time, but Wil said that his knee predicted it was going to be a nice day. He was rarely wrong about the weather. The fire was put out, and the trio started off across the prairie. The first coulee they came to was long and narrow. There were a few scattered clumps of brush, and it seemed that it couldn't hold a thing, but Wil knew better. He told Matt to go around the ridge, and he walked down the middle with the boy. They waited nearly a half hour and started into the coulee. It only took a few minutes, and Matt fired a shot at something. Then all was quiet again. The boy looked up at Poppa, wondering what had happened.

They walked along slowly and then heard another shot, but this time it was more muffled than the last. There just ahead was Matt, standing over a nice young buck. He had taken a quick shot at him and had to chase him down to finish the job. It was a nice deer, but they were a long way from camp.

They finished gutting the buck and started to drag him toward camp. Wil was puffing in no time, and Matt told him that he could handle it by himself. Wil sat for a bit to catch his breath, and Matt took a quick look at him. His color wasn't good at all.

"Take one of those little pills, Wil. It will make you feel a lot better."

Wil did as the doctor ordered, and in a few minutes, his color was back, and he was breathing easier. The boy wasn't aware of what was going on, and they were both glad for it.

"That's some pretty fair medicine, Matt. It makes me feel good right away."

They got back to camp and found a tree to hang the buck in until they headed back home in a couple days. The drag had tired Matt out, and his lunch break was spent laying in the tent resting with little Wil beside him. The afternoon plan was to head in different directions and wait for the last of daylight when the biggest bucks could sometimes be seen. The boy went with Wil, and this time, he was allowed to carry his own rifle. Wil carried his cartridges.

"Can we go now?" asked little Wil.

Poppa looked at him with a big grin and handed him his rifle. Matt headed north and had a good place chosen for the afternoon. He still wanted a chance at that big one that they had seen on the first day in camp.

Wil and the boy headed southwest down an old game trail. Young Wil had no trouble keeping up with his grandpa, and their quick pace ate up a mile in short order. Wil found a place that overlooked the wide end of a large coulee, and there were rocks and stumps enough to make a good shooting rest for his grandson, should the need arise. They piled up a generous amount of wood onto a large rock, and the boy sat down to see if it was the right height for him. It brought a smile to the boy's face, and Wil knew that it would work if needed.

They sat quietly and looked hard at the surrounding plains. They were right on the edge of the coulee, and they could see quite some distance. Young Wil pointed off to the east, and the old man looked hard but couldn't see anything. Age had dimmed his vision some, but the youngster saw a deer way off toward camp. He may have had trouble understanding some things, but he had the eyes of an eagle. Wil convinced him that the deer was too far away, so he kept looking for another one that was closer.

As darkness neared, a large buck appeared down in the draw, feeding its way slowly toward them. It was still over a hundred yards away, and Wil thought to shoot it, but this was a shot that the boy could make, even if the gun was of small caliber. He helped little Wil steady the rifle on the stump. The old man put a shell in the gun for him, and then he aimed long and hard. Wil kept waiting for the shot, but nothing happened. He had decided to shoot it himself and had raised the gun to his shoulder when the boy pulled the trigger. The deer dropped and got right back up. He was running like a freight train right toward them when Wil raised his gun to finish him off for the boy. Just as he got the deer in his sights, the big animal fell and lay still only thirty yards from them.

Neither of them said a word for a moment or two, and then Wil let out a war whoop that could have been heard for miles. The boy smiled as if it were no feat at all. They stood over the deer counting the points, little Wil warming his hand in Poppa's pocket. Wil had loved that boy since way before he was born, but today he looked at him with a different eye. Here was a child that had a life changing handicap, but he fought back and gave his all to something that he could do well. The child had made a heart shot on a moving animal at one hundred yards, something that a lot of good men couldn't do. He never showed any sign of pride or boasting, but he looked at this as something that he could do.

Matt came up and said, "What did you get, Wil?" He looked at the deer. "I never saw one bigger than this before. How far was it?"

The words stuck in Wil's throat, and he had to take a deep breath before starting to tell the story. After a minute or two, Matt reached down and picked up the boy. He hugged him tightly and kissed him on the cheek. Never had there been a time when a family had felt so close. There would be no more talk about what little Wil couldn't do. From now on, they would all concentrate on what he wanted to try and help him develop his own set of skills. He had his own interests, and the family would all help him to achieve what he wanted to accomplish. You had to have some book learning, and everyone knew that, but there were other things that were just as important for a boy like Wil.

The meat pole now held two deer, and they wouldn't need to cut them up before they went home. It would be nice, however, if Wil could get one, but after the boy getting the big buck, he figured that the hunt was a sure success. Matt wondered how his son would react to his first kill, but in his short life, he had learned where meat came from by living next to a working farm.

The next day found Wil starting to break camp. Matt and the boy had headed out early with the car to hunt a spot a few miles away.

Wil took some extra time watching the sunrise and drinking a third cup of coffee. The sky turned crimson red early, and that usually meant a storm soon, but it faded as the sun came up. The air was still, and a lot of hunting birds were coming over headed to the south. Unlike the waterfowl, these birds hunted the whole way down. They used a lot of energy and had to eat nearly every day. A kestrel snatched a small bird from a bush a few feet from Wil's head and settled on the ground to eat his meal. Most of the large birds back home on the river had already gone south, but it was considerably different around here. In this part of the world, you could pour your coffee while looking at a clear sky, and by the time it got cool enough to drink, there were snowflakes falling into the cup. Weather had a way of cleaning out good farmers here, too. Back home you figured an acre and a half for a cow and her calf, but here, you needed at least thirty acres to feed the same animals. Deep snows sometimes cleaned out entire calf crops, too. Life was tough here, but so were the men and women. They made do with what they had and knew adversity from a young age. *These were all good people, though*, thought Wil.

He pulled the center pole from the tent and watched it collapse onto the prairie. The stakes were a different story, as they were firmly stuck into the hard ground. He kicked them all with a sideward blow of his boot and got them out. He packed the stakes, ropes, and poles inside the folded tent and rolled it up firmly making a neat bundle. The food locker was nearly empty, and he filled the space with anything he could find. The fire was always the last to die, and he enjoyed his time alone, sifting through his thoughts.

He thought of a time many years back, when the men made drives on the river ice and, they speared a lot of fish for their families. Sometimes it was a bit dangerous, but they were quite careful. Men stood on the edge of the ice in only a foot or two of water. The others went downstream and made a drive up toward open water and the men with the spears. They hit the ice with large sticks and pushed the fish ahead of them to be speared when they came out from under the ice. Wil thought that it might be fun to show Matt how it was done. It only took about ten men to do it.

Around noon, Matt and little Wil came back to camp empty handed. There was some bread left for sandwiches, so they ate and drank coffee. Even the boy had his cup with the men. They decided that it was time to head back home, and the loading of the car began right away. They were in a hurry to get started on their trip home before the snow came and locked them in for the winter. Matt drove the trailer up to the deer and dropped them into the trailer. The load was covered with a strong canvas, and little Wil jumped into the back seat, covering up with a heavy blanket. In a short while, the boy was sleeping as the car rocked back and forth, headed down the dusty road toward home.

Chapter 31: The Circle of Life

The fall season had passed, and early winter brought heavy snow and extremely cold weather. The store thermometer registered fifty-six below zero one morning, but everyone in the area said that they could remember colder temperatures than that. These were pretty tough people, and it seemed that they thrived on adversity.

Ma celebrated her eightieth birthday, and the whole community gathered at the church to honor her on the big day. Many of her old friends came from the southern part of the state, and she had cousins from all over the area eating birthday cake with her. She was a lovely lady, and the whole community had called on her at one time or another for help. She either brought their children into the world as a midwife or threatened to take them out when they stole her raspberries. Everyone in the area knew her and thought she was pretty special.

Ma posed with Wil in the front of the church for a photograph taken by a traveling salesman. This would hang in the entry of the church for all to see. She also had a picture taken of Matt, Jane, and little Wil to be hung in their cabin. Wil built a good frame for it and placed it over the fireplace.

Christmas time was extra special this year. Ma confided to Matt that she didn't think Wil would make it until spring. He had been having a lot of coughing spells and taking a lot more nitroglycerine. Earlier in the winter, Matt had given Wil some laudanum for the pain, and he noticed that he needed it more frequently. He now figured that Ma needed to know about her husband having lung cancer. He hadn't told Wil yet because he didn't think that he wanted that kind of bad news in his last days. If he kept going as he had, he could still possibly live for a few more months.

The Christmas season brought many gifts, especially for young Wil. It seemed that everyone really liked the boy, and he helped everyone whenever they asked him. He was tough for his age and loved shoveling snow. Santa brought him a new sled and a pair of snow pants. There were the usual family gatherings with way too much food, and it seemed that everyone ate enough to hibernate on.

On one winter day, when the sun was shining brightly, Wil put on his snow shoes and walked through the woods to Matt's cabin. He asked Matt if he wanted to go spear some fish on Saturday. Matt asked about how it was done and thought that it would be a lot of fun.

Wil talked to a few other men, and they decided to meet on Saturday at the general store and bring their spears.

The river, even that late in the winter, was open in places because of the speed that the water flowed. There was always hoarfrost in the trees from the steam coming off the open water. Once in a while, there was an eagle sitting on a branch nearby, hoping to catch a meal of fish, but he was rarely successful. He had a far better chance of catching a careless muskrat.

The men walked downstream a half mile and made a line across the frozen river. Wil and two other men stood on the edge of the ice, staring intently at the dark water. It was less than two feet deep, and there was plenty of ice to stand on. The men advanced toward the open water, pounding on the ice with the butt end of their spears. The man to Wil's left made a quick jab and pulled up a nice walleye. Wil saw a flicker of light in the water and jabbed at another one. He had it flopping on the ice in a moment and was back looking for more. The drivers were only about two hundred feet away, and the fish were coming faster, so they slowed down to let the men with the spears catch up.

Matt looked up to see what kind of fish Wil was getting, and in a time span that covered no more than half a heartbeat, the ice cracked at Wil's feet, and he disappeared under the ice. The men on either side ran over to help him, but he had been pulled under the ice by the strong current. Matt poked at the ice fiercely with his spear and couldn't get through it. Each of the men went at the ice with a strong determination to save their longtime friend.

It was all to no avail. In a very few moments, Matt had lost his long time hunting partner and the best friend he had ever known. He sat down on the ice and cried like a baby. It was all so sudden. One minute, he was smiling holding up his spear with a walleye, and the next, he was gone, as if he had never been there to start with. Matt had seen death hundreds of times and thought of it as a part of life, the end of it. Now, he had to face it so much more closely.

The men were returning from down river after searching for open water to get Wil out. They were all holding their heads low in sorrow. Wil meant so much to every member of the community. He brought them food when times were tough and drank with them when times were good. He attended the birth of many babies and buried a good number of his friends.

Old Wil's body was never recovered, but the following spring, there was a memorial service on the bank of the Bigfork River where Matt and Jane had gotten married. Matt eulogized his friend to all and told of the many things that he had been taught by the old man. Young Wil stood beside Ma and placed his hand in her pocket. He was still having a hard time understanding what had happened to Poppa. Where had he gone? All he knew was that he was missing, and it hurt really bad.

The preacher said a few words of comfort to the family, and each person went his or her own way. A man came into the world, touched the lives of many, and left.

Epilogue

I sit tonight looking out my window at the river. The feeling of urgency to get it all down on paper is starting to ease some. Outside in the warm summer night air, the river still splashes and churns in the darkness.

Many years have passed since the death of my friend Wil, and Jane has given me two more lovely children, a boy and a girl. Little Wil has a place of his own on the river near Poppa's cabin, and he farms and hunts the land as his namesake had done.

Ma was buried between her favorite apple tree and the raspberry patch, and the river continues its journey northward to the ocean.

Check out these other
Great Books by Ron Shepherd

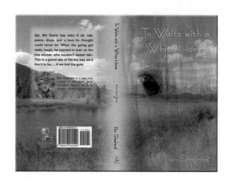

For More information on these books
and any upcoming books visit us at www.ronshepherd.com

Ron Shepherd has a new book, *"**Brothers by Fire**"* coming out in mid-year 2006. It's a tale of two boys, one white and one Anishinaabe, who were raised by a school teacher in the Great White Oak area in the 1930's. They spend their adult lives searching for one another.

This book along with the other three were published by Global Video Marketing, publishing division. If you would like to send us a review on any of his books please do so at globalvideomarketing@helloworld.com. We appreciate any comments, questions, or interest in any of the books.

Would you like to have Ron Shepherd speak at community events, corporate seminars, or educational institutions? Or, would you like Ron to come to your community for a book signing? If so, please send your request to stevemayer@helloworld.com. We look forward to hearing from you.

Interested in self-publishing your book? We have the know how to get you there. From designing a professional cover to getting your book around the world. The Global Way makes it simple for you. Please contact us at:

Global Video Marketing
Attn: Publishing Division
7529 Libke Road
P.O. Box 337
Side Lake, MN 55781